The Immortal Boy

The Immortal Boy

Francisco Montaña Ibañéz

TRANSLATED BY DAVID BOWLES

LQ

LEVINE QUERIDO

MONTCLAIR · AMSTERDAM · NEW YORK

For Amparo, the mommy
For Matías and Violeta

.

This is an Em Querido book
Published by Levine Querido

LQ
LEVINE QUERIDO

www.levinequerido.com • info@levinequerido.com
Levine Querido is distributed by Chronicle Books LLC
Text copyright © 2008 by Francisco Montaña Ibáñez
Translation copyright © 2021 by David Bowles
Originally published in Colombia by Babel Libros
Library of Congress Control Number: 2020937502
ISBN 978-1-64614-044-2
Printed and bound in China

Published March 2021
FIRST PRINTING

At such hours,

people and things behave

like those little props and figurines,

carved from the wood of elder trees

and kept in a glazed tinfoil box,

which become electrically charged

by rubbing against the glass and

are drawn at every movement

into the most unusual

relationships. . . .

In streams like

curtains of rain,

presents fall

upon the child—

presents that veil

the world from him.

—WALTER BENJAMIN
On Hashish

HE DOOR WASN'T LOCKED. David pushed at it, and it swung open easily, like it wanted him inside. He walked into the room, approached the table where the gas stove sat, sniffed at a pot, and turned away wincing. The room was empty except for Hector and Manuela—tucked into her drawer—both of them asleep. Since he needed his older brother Hector, David just stood there, waiting for him to wake up, letting his gaze wander over the handful of objects in the room. The two beds where the older kids slept. The drawer where Manuela, the youngest of the five siblings, hardly fit anymore. The table where they cooked, ate, and did their homework. A few cardboard boxes stuffed with clothes.

Before he left, their father had rented the rest of the house to Doña Yeni. This room was all they needed, he'd told them.

David liked to imagine the table was his. Once, there had been a decal in his lollipop wrapper and he'd stuck it to the underside of the table, marking his property. Now he ran his fingers over its edges, upturned by this daily ritual, making sure it was still in place. He shifted his gaze toward Manuela. The little girl had opened her eyes, and she looked at him silently, sucking on the edge of her blanket. He had always loved her special. She was pretty and small, like a miniature mother. He was about to say hi when his stomach twisted with the same pain that had kept him from school the entire last week.

As soon as the cramp loosened its grip, he decided to start staring at Hector. Oddly enough, though David didn't know exactly how or why, when he stared at a sleeping person, they always woke up. It was as if by looking at them he touched them, as if he dropped an invisible weight.

His brother Hector was no exception. He opened sleep-blurred eyes and hissed, recognizing the gaze boring into him.

"Hector," David whispered.

His brother turned away and covered his head with the blankets.

"Hector," the boy repeated, shaking him carefully, mindful of what could happen. "Hector."

"Oh, what the—! Let me sleep!" Hector growled. He poked his head out of the blankets and turned just enough to look at him. "What's wrong with you, David?"

"Don't be like that, Hector. It's just . . . my tummy doesn't hurt so bad anymore."

"Well, congratulations," the older boy muttered, covering his head again.

"The boarder sent you a message." David pulled the blanket from Hector's head.

Hector sat up on his elbows and shouted at him like a wounded bull.

"I need to sleep! Can't it wait?"

"It's just that . . . I'm hungry," the younger boy confessed, sounding embarrassed.

"Well, eat what's in the pot!" Hector replied, irritated.

"But she said I can't keep eating rotten stuff."

Hector surged to his feet and pushed his brother to the floor. "And, what, it's rotten?" Manuela closed her eyes and covered her head with her blanket.

"Yes, it is. I get it now," David continued, undaunted, from the floor. "Doña Yeni taught me to tell what stuff's rotten by the way it smells. Eating nasty things gives me a tummy ache. . . . What do I do, Hector? I'm hungry, and Maria doesn't get back until really late."

Hector sniffed at the pot and then glared at it, struggling against the desire to smash it over his brother's head. The boy needed to handle things by himself!

"Fine, here!" he said through his teeth, throwing a wadded bill at David. "Go on, see what you can buy with that. If you're lucky, somebody will give you some soup to fix you up, so you can get back to school."

David picked the money up from the floor and stood, stepping away from his brother's fury.

"And take the girl," Hector added, submerging himself in the blankets again.

David took Manuela's hand, helped her put on her shoes, and gently took the blanket from her, all in silence, taking care not to lose sight of his brother who was breathing heavily in the bed. He smoothed his sister's dress and saw the look on her face. She was waiting patiently, happy at the idea of going out. When he was about to open the door, he heard one last shout:

"And give your sister some of whatever they give you! Don't come back until I'm awake! You hear me, you empty-headed brat?"

Manuela looked up at David, smiling like his little

partner in crime. She knew they were about to do something mischievous, so she dragged him out of the room.

""""

"GIVE HIM THAT BAG OF POTATOES," said the big man who never stooped, even under the weight of two heavy bundles. He gestured for the dirt-covered Hector to approach the truck and grab one.

"Way to go, kid," the dockworker congratulated him as he dropped the bag on his shoulder and made sure he could handle it. "Now, take that inside," he challenged the teen.

Hector took a breath and carried the bundle into the warehouse, step by step. Once inside, the big man showed him where to lay it down.

"Still got the carrots to go. Come on."

Hector followed him to the truck and hefted another bag onto his shoulder. He no longer noticed the ache in his back. Streams of sweat made furrows in the dirt that covered his face and neck. He tried to wipe his forehead with a sleeve, but it was already soaked, so all he ended up doing was smear the liquid that poured from his body.

He carried ten more bundles into the warehouse. When the truck was finally empty, he sat on one of the last ones. As he caught his breath, Hector dug a hole into the side of the bag. His fingers fumbled with the organic threads. He squeezed one in first, then two, and then he felt the cabuya fiber give way, letting his whole hand through. He reached around till he found one of the potatoes.

He wrapped his fingers around it for a moment, but then he just pulled out his hand, leaving the spud where it was. Instead, he sipped water from a plastic bag the big man had thrown at him.

From an aisle in the warehouse, two women who were organizing goods on the shelves looked his way.

"Why do you keep staring at him?" the older asked the younger.

"Look at him. He's only been here for a month, and he already seems older," the younger answered.

"Whatever. He's still a boy."

The women fell silent. They kept pulling bags of rice and beans from cardboard boxes, arranging them on shelves, until the older one stopped, sighed, and whispered as she pointed at Hector.

"Do you like him?"

The girl smiled, blushing, and ran a sleeve over her forehead.

"You're right. He's pretty young," she said.

"Well, so are you! How old do you think he is?" the woman asked.

"Seventeen?"

"Not even close," she said, resuming her work. "Thir-teen. *Maybe.* He just looks older."

"I guess it's because he had to start working so young . . ."

"Yeah, like we all did. How old are *you*, anyway?"

The girl blushed again and stared at a row of bags full of red seeds.

"What difference does it make to you?"

Hector, who had caught his breath, noticed the blush on the girl's cheeks and felt her gaze search out his own, for the briefest of moments, when no one but the two of them could see.

2

T HURTS TO HAVE your face smooshed against a
wall. But I'm not sure what hurts more: the anger
you feel when you can't defend yourself, or the pain of your
bones getting pressed against the bricks. And this time, I
couldn't have moved even if I'd tried. Three of them had
ahold of me. One had my arms twisted at my back, the other
was grabbing my legs, almost lifting me off the ground,
and the other was pushing my face against the wall. They
threatened me so I wouldn't scream. To be honest, I would've
anyway, but I literally couldn't. I could barely *breathe* my face
was so smooshed against those bricks. I don't know how long

I was like that, crying in anger, while the three bullies insulted and shook me. But that boy showed up and scared them good. Who knows how he did it. He looks younger than them. Maybe he's like me, small for his age. But I think they're already afraid of him, so all it took was a couple of kicks and a yell from him and they left me alone.

When they let go of me and I could breathe again, I felt so dizzy that I fell down right there in the corridor. I didn't faint, I just couldn't move. It was like someone yanked out my bones. The boy stared and then made a gun with his hand, pointing at me like he was going to shoot. But when the director showed and found me lying on the floor, he disappeared. They picked me up on a stretcher and took me to the infirmary. The nurse told me that I was fine. She cleaned the scratches they'd left on my forehead and my legs and asked me if I knew who'd hit me. I didn't have any idea who the jerks were, so I came off as tough because I wouldn't snitch. The lady calmed me down and explained that kids do that sort of thing to newbies. Later they all become friends.

After a while the nurse let me go. As soon as I got outside, I started looking for the boy. But this place is huge. I think it used to be a plantation, and now the big house is all the offices and a small dining room. The girls' dorm is a building attached to the house. The school is on the other side, past the football field, the library, the laboratories, and the cafeteria. I couldn't find him anywhere. I headed behind the girls' dorm, along the path through the orchard. I'd never gone that way, but I discovered that at the far edge of the orchard, the path ends in a wall. Maybe it used to go right past the ditch that's in front of the wall, heading into the fields on the other side. I'm guessing there didn't used to be a wall around this whole place. But now the path ends a few steps before it. And there I saw him, huddled under a willow, next to the ditch. I didn't mean to bother him, but when I walked up and touched his shoulder, he leapt up like a wild animal, shouting insults and running off. All I wanted to do was find out his name and thank him.

When he was far enough away, he turned toward me and fired a bunch of times with his hand. I wasn't sure what to do, but since he kept shooting, I figured the best thing was to play dead, so I dropped to the ground. He holstered his hand in one pocket and walked away.

3

HECTOR WAS, IN FACT, thirteen years old. He stared at the ceiling with his hands under his head, not blinking. He did not see what was before his eyes. He was simply elsewhere. His legs pedaled hard, he lifted the back tire of his bike, spinning it like a top. In front of him, the young woman from the warehouse lifted her gaze from the floor. Her eyes met his so subtly that only he could perceive the slight blush he brought to her cheeks.

"Leave her alone, already!" demanded Maria. She was the older sister. She was speaking to Robert, the third youngest of the siblings, and to David, the second youngest. They were chasing Manuela through the room, pinching her butt to make her scream and jump. All that noise and commotion were keeping her from finishing what she was cooking on the stove.

"I said leave her alone! You're going to make her cry!" Maria shouted, stopping them with the intensity of her voice and the fierceness of her eyes. She held a knife in one hand, and she glared at her brothers as if she might hurl herself at them.

"Enough, Maria!" Hector warned in a low voice, emerging from his daydreams.

"She's always shouting at us," David complained. Manuela nodded.

"She's nuts," Robert clarified. He dropped to the ground dramatically, throwing himself onto his back.

"Just stop shouting at them. I can't even think."

"And she won't let us play," said Manuela, pushing her tummy out.

"What is it you're thinking about, huh, Hector?" Maria cut back. "You never help, you don't even notice I'm exhausted. After school, Mrs. Carmen had me handle all the sales at the store."

"Did she pay you?" He was suddenly interested.

"She gave me two pounds of rice and beans. What do you think we're eating tonight?"

Maria began shrieking again at the children, who had restarted their horseplay, this time throwing themselves on top of Robert, who was still lying on the floor, worn out. The little ones fell silent when Maria slammed the pots and growled words that nobody understood. Manuela stared at her and mocked her in silence. Robert and David covered their mouths to stop from bursting with laughter. Hector kept making his invisible bicycle fly in the empty space in front of his eyes.

4

THEY PUT US IN GROUPS BY AGE, not grade level or ability. In my group, there were fifteen of us. Some couldn't even read or write, and others had totally forgotten how. The only sure thing was that none of us had anywhere else to go. Some kids prayed that their parents would show up one day to claim them. Others had already given up on that idea. Many figured that even though they were getting older, some couple would come by and adopt them. As for me, I hoped my parents would get out of jail. There were some kids who liked being on the streets. Not me. I preferred my own house, but between this place and the street? This was better. I think lots of the kids I spoke with felt the same.

But none of them knew anything about the boy who saved me from the three bullies.

"He's a newbie, almost as new as you. He's nine years old," one said.

"He don't speak to nobody. Just shoots," said another. But I already knew that.

"They call him the Immortal Boy," said the first kid, very quietly, like he was revealing a dangerous secret. "Bullets can't kill him."

I stared at him without getting what he meant. What I needed was to know the boy's *name*. I'd been trying to get close enough to ask, but he always ran from me like I had cooties. Sometimes, when we passed each other in the dining room, or in one of the classrooms in the library, he would look at me and shoot with his hand.

"He sees the shrink every day," said an older girl, rolling her eyes at the boy who'd mentioned the whole immortality thing. She visited the woman just as often; she was not the kind of girl to babble about stuff she didn't know.

Me? I did *not* pay regular visits the psychologist. Instead, I went to music class, dance class, theater class. I also worked in the garden and in the kitchen. So I asked what you had to do to go see the shrink. If I could set up a visit, maybe she would tell me things about my little savior and explain the best way to get to know him. That's what psychologists are for, right?

"You've got to have some problem, a glitch. Something wrong with your head. Like, it's hard for me to stop digging this hole in my thigh," the girl explained, lifting her skirt and showing me an open wound.

"What happened to you?"

"I pinch myself, without even noticing."

"Doesn't it hurt?" I asked, a little freaked out.

"Not when I'm doing it, no. Later? Yeah, it burns. Sometimes it starts to stink."

I gave her thigh another glance before she covered it again with her skirt. There was no way I was going to pinch a hole in any part of my body.

Nobody knew anything else. I learned that almost everyone feared him, even if he was sort of a protector, because he defended kids with so much violence that even those he saved were afraid. Apparently one time he smashed up the face of some bully. Lots of kids kept repeating that he was the Immortal Boy, that bullets couldn't kill him. Several said he was crazy. Others claimed that he was just weird. And some swore he was from another planet. They were joking, of course. When I saw him, he was always alone, playing with imaginary things and shooting. Several times I followed him as he walked down the short path that ended at the ditch, but as soon as he realized I was following him, he would run back to the building, shooting.

Whether he was immortal, a bully, or just plain weird, I was sure of one thing.

No matter how often he got away from me, one day I was going to catch him and make him my friend.

5

ANUELA HAD ALREADY sucked the four corners of her wool blanket and was getting started on the middle when someone burst in, almost breaking down the door. It was her brother Robert. His nose was bleeding, and one of his eyes was swollen shut. The little girl jumped out of her drawer and ran to look at him more closely.

"What happened?" she asked, pointing at his face.

"Some guys beat me up," Robert muttered. "I didn't do anything, but they jumped me."

He dropped his hand from his nose. It spouted a thick stream of blood.

Manuela covered her face with her hands. "Robert, are you going to die?"

"I don't know," Robert confessed, pinching his nose again. "Bring me a rag."

The girl dropped her damp blanket and found a rag next to the pots.

"Get it wet," Robert instructed. The girl obeyed. He took it from her and held it to his eye.

"Ah, better," he said, relieved.

"You're not going to die now?" asked Manuela.

"I don't know," Robert repeated. Stumbling, he made his way outside to the sink and thrust his head under the open faucet. "But I'm not going back to school."

"Then I can go instead," said his sister behind him. "I don't want to stay here alone." She picked up a eucalyptus seed and threw it at a sky blocked by the leafy branches of trees, in the same pointless way her older brothers always did.

"Sure. You go right ahead. See if they don't smash your face in too," Robert challenged her, smoothing his wet hair and squeezing his nose with the rag.

Offended, Manuela went back inside, picked up her blanket, and started sucking again. She stared at Robert, not knowing what to do with him when he staggered through the door, sniffing loudly.

"Oh, Manuela, don't look at me like that. Nobody's going to touch you. If they do, you come tell me. I'm going to train with this one guy, and then those jerks will learn just who Robert is. Sound good?"

The girl nodded while still sucking the blanket.

"So you're not going to die?" she asked after a while. Her brother had sat down on one of the beds.

"No, I don't think so," he replied. He checked and found his nosebleed had stopped. He pressed the damp rag against his face. "But I can't see anything out of this eye; maybe I'm going blind?"

Manuela walked over and looked at him. His eyelid was mottled and red. At the corner there was a blood clot, and the swelling kept him from opening it. But Manuela saw that, under all that mess, his eye twitched about like a healthy animal.

"Don't worry, Robert. That'll go away." She offered him one edge of her wet blanket. The boy accepted it, and they sat together on the bed, waiting.

〰️

"WHAT DO YOU MEAN, you're not going back to school?" asked Hector.

"If I go back, they'll kill me," Robert explained. "They warned me. Besides, it's better I stay and take care of Manuela."

Manuela pressed tighter against his side. The two hadn't moved in several hours.

"Can I get some more?" David asked. He had finished his soup.

"No. Robert still hasn't served himself," said Maria. "He has to eat something because with that beating—"

"But I'm hungry," David whined.

"What are you going to eat?" Hector asked Robert. "If you don't go back to school, what are you going to eat?"

Robert looked at Maria, realized that his sister was thin and pale. His hands fell to the sides of his body as if he could no longer.

"But I'm telling you they'll beat me up again," Robert complained.

"I'll protect you," David offered. "Nobody messes with me, they know what'll happen to them. Just point them out to me tomorrow, and I'll take care of them."

Hector smiled and patted his head.

"But give me your soup, yeah?" David added.

Robert turned his head to look down at Manuela.

She pushed him away and took back the blanket they had been sharing.

6

I WAS BORED WITH NOTHING to do, so suddenly I found myself in front of the psychologist's office. It was time for her daily sessions, and three kids sat there waiting. None of them was the boy who'd saved me, but one was the girl who dug at her thigh. She saw me, lifted her skirt, and showed me a bandage covering the wound.

"You don't scratch anymore?" I asked.

"Well, yeah, but it's harder with the bandage, so I realize I'm pinching myself and I stop digging my nail in."

"Mind if I join you?" I asked her. She nodded, so I sat

next to her and glanced at the other two boys who were silently waiting for their turn with the doctor.

"What's it like?" I asked, just to see who'd answer.

The boys looked at each other and smiled.

"Who's in there right now?" I added, hoping it was him.

"Julian," said the younger boy. "The one who shoots all the time."

"His name is David," the older boy corrected.

"David?" I exclaimed excitedly as the girl began to pick the skin at the edge of the bandage.

"Yeah, David. I mean, that's what they say," explained the younger boy. "Nobody really knows. He doesn't speak to anybody."

"He arrived a little while ago," the older boy confirmed. "Have you heard what kids keep saying about him?"

I could pretty much guess what was coming, but I told him to go on.

"That he's immortal. Bullets don't kill him," the older boy revealed with a grin.

"That's why he doesn't speak," the younger boy said.

"What do you mean?" I asked, confused.

The girl and the older boy shrugged, but the little kid looked at me like there were letters scrawled all over my face. He motioned me closer.

"Because if he speaks, he might reveal his secret," he whispered in my ear.

"What secret?" I murmured in his ear.

"The secret of his immortality . . ."

The boy pulled away and looked at me, all serious.

"He's a real weirdo. Always hungry," the girl added with a smile. "That's all he ever says—'I'm hungry.'"

None of the news I had just received mattered to me as much as the name of my savior and future friend. My mind repeated it over and over. I was getting ready to ask something else when the door banged open and David came bursting out in a fury, his face red, panting so hard and loud that even when he'd reached the other end of the hallway, he still sounded like some huge, enraged animal. At least to me. I couldn't take my eyes off his heaving back, trying to read in his movements some hint about this boy who had become my obsession. I was so distracted watching him sway back and forth that I didn't notice the doctor had walked over and was looking at me curiously. The two boys nudged each other, smiling, and the girl finally sank her nails into her skin, releasing the slight moisture that circulates beneath.

"What is your name, miss?" the psychologist asked, startling me, just as the others had been hoping.

"Excuse me?" I replied, confused. She was the first person to be so formal with me in this place.

"Your name, dear. What do they call you?"

"Nina," I answered. I glanced at her green eyes and then fixed mine on the floor.

"How long has it been since you arrived?" she continued.

"Two weeks," I replied, afraid she'd scold me. Recently they'd been getting after me for nearly everything I did. I figured it was their way of teaching me how things worked here.

"I haven't seen you, Miss Nina," the woman said, touching my cheek and then making me look up at her. I liked looking into her eyes. "Anytime you want to come chat, please do. My name is Marcela. I'm the psychologist. I'm here to help you children."

"I can come talk to you?" I asked, surprised. I had no idea I could just come. I figured I needed to be shooting people or making myself bleed before she would see me.

"Of course! All you need is something you want to discuss, something that worries you. Shall I expect you one of these days, dear?" she asked, letting go of my chin and smiling.

"Okay," I said excitedly. No one in this place had ever treated me like this. "I'll come tomorrow."

"Not tomorrow. Monday afternoon, after school. Shall I wait for you then?"

I nodded, and realized that my cheeks were burning. Heck, I was sweating all over. The doctor gestured at the girl with the bandage, and the two of them entered the office.

"Wait—you really want to come see her?" asked the older boy, terrified.

I didn't answer. There was something I needed to do.

I ran toward the end of the hallway where David's back had disappeared.

7

THE BAGS OF CARROTS WERE not the most comfortable but certainly the only place where they could hide for a few moments from the eyes of the big man, who could not stand to see his employees resting during business hours. So it was there, in that corner, where Hector and the young woman agreed to meet and chat.

Hector was the first to arrive, pretending to need a bit of air. He sat down, wiped the sweat from his forehead, and tasted the dirt on his lips. His face, his clothes, and his hands were completely covered by a thick, consistent layer of dirt. Once his breathing had slowed, he made sure no one was looking at him, then reached into the nearly invisible pocket of his filthy pants and took out two sticks of gum. He unwrapped one and began to chew it slowly, letting the orange flavor fill his mouth.

"Why did you take so long?" asked the young woman when she arrived. She sat next to him and brushed her hair behind her ears with her fingers. Hector handed her the other stick of gum and stared first at her bare neck and then her ear with its large earring. She put the gum in her mouth and touched his hand, smiling. At that warm contact, Hector became suddenly aware of the roughness of his own skin. He quickly pulled his hand away. The young woman pushed her hair behind her ear again, letting it show. She stared at him.

"I said, why were you late . . . ?"

"I couldn't get here any earlier," Hector replied simply, and kept on chewing.

The young woman got close to his ear and whispered:

"What do you think I called you for?"

Hector could feel her sweet, clean breath on his face. He shrugged in response. The young woman took his hand again. This time Hector just let her. He stared at her lips. They were thin and pale. He was strangely fascinated by her oval face and white skin. As long as she had his dirty, blistered hand in hers, he couldn't stop staring at that face, those intense eyes.

"Why don't you say anything?" she continued.

"I have nothing to say," Hector replied, pulling his hand from the warm prison.

"I do. That's why I called you over. I wanted to know if you'd help me with something."

"Sure, whatever you need."

"Let's take all the cash out of the register and run away."

"Are you kidding?"

"What, you think they treat us well here?"

Hector shrugged again.

"Well, I don't. I'm going to steal what I can. Today."

The young woman's green eyes shone brightly. Hector remembered that he had not finished organizing the bags of chard and that he had a pending delivery. The young woman smacked her gum, waiting for Hector to say something.

"Well, if you don't want to, it's your loss. We could have run off together, to some warmer place; with that money we could've opened a little roadside business, nobody telling us what to do. Doesn't that sound nice?" she whispered.

Hector nodded and let her fold her warm hands around his once more. He sighed, spit his gum out, and stood up.

"I can't," he muttered, heading slowly toward the vege-table section, where he was greeted by the shout of the big man asking why he had taken so long.

""""

"HELLO," THE WOMAN SAID, peeking her head through the open door of the one-room apartment. Robert set his carrot down and walked toward her.

"What happened to you, boy?" she asked when she saw Robert's black eye. He did not answer and instead stared at her with his good one. "I'm here to talk about the rent."

"Yeah?" asked Robert.

"And you? How's your belly doing?" she asked David, changing the subject as she entered the room.

"Better, Doña Yeni, thank you," said the younger boy, shrinking just a little at the presence of an adult.

"So what about the rent?" Robert prompted her.

"I don't have the money to pay you. . . . I wanted to see if you'd let me stay . . ."

Robert turned to his siblings. Manuela held a carrot in one hand and her blanket in the other. David stared at her, speechless, his eyes wide. Robert thought it wasn't fair for her to stay in their house without paying rent, but he also knew that the woman had helped David and had taken care of Manuela. Besides, he supposed that if she left, it would be difficult to find another adult to board in the house with them.

"Well, okay," Robert said without moving from the door. "But help us out with food."

David's eyes lit up. Manuela sucked contentedly on her blanket, and the three children stared at the woman. She remained silent for a moment.

"It's better if I wash your clothes," she said at last, glancing around.

"And you have to give us food. We're hungry," Robert insisted.

"When I can," the woman said, shaking her head. "Whenever I have some, I'll share it with you. That and much more, now that we're like a family."

The three children glanced at each other, confused.

"You didn't know?"

"What?" asked Robert and David at the same time.

"Before he left, your dad asked me to look after you," the woman replied as she began to collect dirty clothes throughout the room, pulling the sheets off the beds and using them to wrap it all up. "I'm going to wash this for you."

She moved toward the door, but stopped when she saw that Manuela and David were sitting on a bag of carrots. "And what's that?"

"Hector brought it," Manuela said proudly, "so we have something to eat."

"Ah, that's perfect!" the woman exclaimed, shifting the bundle of clothes to one arm and grabbing a bunch of carrots with her free hand. "I'll make you some soup in a jiffy."

Manuela cheered, but Robert's hot glare burned into her.

"Put potatoes in it," he demanded. "Or don't bother."

The woman, already at the door, looked down at him and exclaimed:

"Just like his dad, this one!"

And Robert watched her leave toward the laundry room.

8

I DIDN'T THINK WE WERE the same, David and me. I just liked him a lot. I don't know why. But from the moment I saw him and he saved me from those bullies, I couldn't get him out of my head. I kept dreaming about walking through the garden with him. In the dream there was no wall: right after the ditch, the path continued alongside the pastures. We were holding hands as we walked. That was what I'd been imagining, so I told the psychologist. Other kids warned me it was better not to tell her anything, because whatever I said went into my file.

But she seemed like good people to me and I figured I could share stuff with her.

"Why don't you tell him that, dear?" she asked, smiling.

"Well, because he won't let me," I replied, choking up. "The minute he sees me, he runs off. I know where he likes to hang out now, but when I show up, he drops everything and hides. I don't know what he's doing out there, anyway."

"'Out there' where?" The woman was interested.

"Near the ditch, behind the garden, beside the willows," I said. Then I worried I had betrayed him by revealing what had taken me so many days to discover. Maybe that hideaway was one of his secrets. I remained silent for a moment until the psychologist continued:

"And in the dream, there is no wall?"

I shook my head and asked, suddenly scared:

"Is he going to get in trouble?"

I had heard that consequences in this place were terrible and usually unfair. Once a kid in front of me in the lunch line dropped his tray of food and ran back to ask for more. The rest of us just stepped over the mess, without a word, until someone started whining about how gross it was to see mashed potatoes and Jello all smashed together like brains on the floor. A couple of others stopped and made even nastier comments until the teacher in charge noticed the spill and forced the closest boy to clean it up even though it wasn't his fault. Another kid, with a reputation for being absent-minded, was sent to clean the toilets because he kept staring out the window. Everybody said worse things could happen, horrible punishments that luckily I never saw, but that made me afraid for him, first because I didn't want anything to happen to him, and second because if he knew the punishment was my fault, any hope we might talk one day would completely disappear.

"No, don't worry. He's not in any trouble."

The woman looked at the clock and asked:

"Would you like to talk about anything else, Miss Nina? We have half an hour."

I shrugged and looked at her. I didn't know what to talk about. Or, I mean, I didn't know where to start.

"I don't know," I said.

"For example, maybe your mother?" she suggested.

I felt a hole open up in my stomach. If I let it get any bigger, I wouldn't be able to stop crying for days, I knew it.

"My mom's in jail. I don't like to talk about her," I said, getting up.

"Ah, don't worry, you don't have to leave, dear. We can listen to music."

She slid a CD into the stereo. Out poured the most

beautiful, saddest music I had ever heard in my life. Notes from a piano, maybe played by a child. It wasn't anything fancy: just simple and moving.

"Do you like it?" she asked.

I nodded. I couldn't speak. If I spoke, I would release a flow of tears, and days ago I had sworn never to cry again.

"It's Bach, Johann Sebastian Bach," she explained, as if I should know that man. "He died a long time ago, but he left this beautiful music. I love putting it on when I want to concentrate."

She leaned back against her chair to think about who knows what, maybe what David was doing near the ditch, or maybe something else.

I kept thinking about the time my mom bought me that pink dress for my birthday party. I was very excited. It's weird, but I almost didn't remember the party or the gifts or the friends. I remembered that afterward, when we were alone, she had hugged me and one of her earrings had gotten caught on a button of my dress. Not knowing this, I jumped with excitement, yanking the earring and tearing her ear. Blood splattered my face and neck, and my mom screamed at me, because of the pain, I'm sure. I was so scared, but after she had pressed a handkerchief, which quickly turned red, to her ear, she apologized and hugged me. My head was pressed against her belly and I could feel her heart pumping rivers of blood and I wanted to keep listening forever.

"It's time," said Marcela, interrupting my thoughts as she turned off the music. "See you next week?

I nodded and went out into the hallway. At the end, staring at the door I was walking through, stood David. As soon as he saw me, he smiled.

"Hey," I said and walked toward him. He stopped smiling. When I was close enough, he dropped a berry in my hand. I felt the moist skin of the fruit and looked at it in wonder. When I looked up to ask him what I should do with it, he was gone. His back was all I saw, swallowed up by the stairwell.

I knew there was no point in chasing him, so I stepped out onto a balcony and stared at La Valvanera, that white chapel that sits on the hilltop of Cerro de la Cruz, while the wind tugged at me.

I looked down at the deep red berry, and without hesitation, I ate it.

9

THIEF," THE BIG MAN GROWLED, pushing him. Hector fell back against bags of carrots, covering his face.

"I didn't do anything," he groaned.

"Liar. I saw you with that slut! After all those bags of food I gave you! Ungrateful little . . ."

"But I didn't do anything."

"Well, double whammy: no bread and no cheese, either. Now get out of here! You're lucky I don't call the police on you."

The big man lifted him bodily and threw Hector out the door. After a brief flight, he slammed painfully into the pavement. When he could breathe again, Hector got up slowly and started walking away from the warehouse. He didn't know where to go, so he simply wandered toward the river.

There were just a few houses nearby, their clay shingles a random cluster of red blobs. He crossed some fields and sat down in the ravine to watch the thick black water swirling with gray foam. It seemed more like tar than water, and its smell would have normally run anyone off who wanted to protect their noses and lungs from contamination. But Hector didn't care about such things. He needed to forget his aching body and decide what to do next. The sluggish movement of the water helped him relax, and before long he stopped noticing the smell. He forgot his bruises too, and after a while, he was thinking clearly. Although he got paid next to nothing in the warehouse, they gave him food. He was able to take something home to his siblings by the time they got home from school. It wasn't much, but it was enough so that they didn't go to bed on an empty stomach. The most obvious next step was to get another job. That was the first thing. When his father returned, Hector could then prove he had been able to take care of his brothers and sisters. He thought about the young woman's green eyes, her warm hands wrapping around his, and the hard line of her lips when she had tried to make him her accomplice. He imagined that if he had gone with her, maybe now he would be sitting beside a pool and not a polluted river, his body broken. He remembered the fresh, clean smell that came from her lips and had to rub his hand over his face to escape the memory. He had acted well. He had no regrets. There was a task to complete, and he was going to complete it no matter what.

Hector got up slowly, mastering every muscle of his battered legs, and headed back up the hill. The slope made the road seem very long. Each step reawakened a bruise. He finally reached the park in his neighborhood and eased down onto one of the benches. A new ache reminded him he had not eaten anything all day besides the aguapanela his sister Maria had made before going to school. The surge from that was long gone. Hector took deep breaths and tried to ignore the rumbling. He stared at the basketball court, the children's games, the tree, and the exercise bars.

A whistle came, from one corner of the park, it seemed. Hector got up and looked that way. Another whistle. He turned to the opposite corner. The whistles kept echoing from all the streets that led to the park, until the guys appeared. He smiled when he saw them.

"What're you doing here? What happened to you?" said the one who wore a leather jacket over his bare torso. The others jerked their heads in greeting.

"Work. They threw me out."

"The fat dude?" asked the one in the jacket.

"Yeah."

"With neighbors like that, huh? Am I right or am I right?" continued the guy with the jacket. "That's why the dude only hires street rats from the other side of town."

"And he beat the crap out of you?" asked the one with a turtleneck sweater that at some point had been white. Hector nodded, running his hand over the scraped arm he showed them. The boy snapped his fingers, impressed.

"But did you at least get back at him? Steal some good stuff?" asked the turtleneck guy.

"No. Didn't get a chance." Hector sighed and remembered the young woman, the throbbing vein in her neck, her green eyes burning.

"Poor, toothless piranha," another said, cackling. The others joined in.

"I need work," Hector whispered.

"Hey, why don't you head over to Julio's and see what he can do?" said the one in the leather jacket.

"Julio?"

"Yeah, dude's pretty decent. Maybe he'll help you out too . . ."

※※※

"THE PUNK WAS HUNGRY!" exclaimed the woman, taking the plate from the table. Hector was still clutching the spoon. He wiped his mouth with his dirty sleeve and looked at his benefactor. The heat from the soup had spread through his body and helped wash away the remnants of the beating. Julio, though just a few years older than Hector, was smiling at him as if welcoming a son returned from a long journey.

"Let's see, punk." He leaned forward on his elbows, staring at him. "What do you know how to do, then?"

"Anything. I'll do whatever needs doing," replied Hector, feeling a little dizzy from eating so fast.

"Right on, that's the attitude. Not gonna let them step on us, right?"

Hector smiled in response.

"You're one of those guys who takes care of his people!" Julio insisted. "Tough as nails. Dedicated to your brothers and sisters. Know what I mean?" He turned to the woman who had taken the plate away and was now opening two sodas behind the dark wooden counter. The woman nodded and walked over to them, bottles in hand. "Do you like Colombiana? It's the only soda I drink. Champagne of colas."

Hector nodded.

"But hey, let's get down to business, right?

"Yeah. I need a job," Hector reiterated.

"I'm going to help you." Julio took a deep breath and looked him in the eyes until the atmosphere grew serious. "But right now? I got nothing. Don't get me wrong, though: just wait a few days, and something will come up."

Hector stared at him, desperate.

"For the time being," Julio went on, holding his eyes, "here's a gift."

He pulled out a wad of fifty-thousand-peso bills. Peeling two off, he handed them to Hector.

"So you can see that I've got your back, yeah?"

Hector looked down at the bills, not daring to touch them.

"It's a lot of money," he said cautiously. It was more than most people made in a week.

"That's nothing. We're gonna touch the sky with our hands." Smiling, Julio set the money down in front of

Hector. Then he frowned. "You can pay me back later if you want, but right now, accept it. Relax. Take food home. Come on, do it."

Hector stood, holding on to the chair to keep from falling. The woman behind the counter was grinning at him.

"Cool, kid. Get moving," said Julio, and he took out his cell phone, which had started to ring.

EVERY TIME HE SHOT ME I DIED, even if we were far apart. He'd look at me, point, and shoot, making a sound I couldn't hear, though the instant I saw his lips moving, I'd fall dead no matter where we were. But that day, I was in the garden making sure there weren't any slugs or other creepy crawlers on the bushes. I looked up to wipe the sweat from my forehead and saw him on the other side. I stared at him. Surely he noticed, because as if feeling the warmth of my gaze, he whirled around. I expected him to shoot me, so I was already figuring out the best way to fall dead without smashing the lettuces that were barely emerging from the soil. But instead, he started walking toward me. My heart started beating wildly, and I felt like I was running out of breath. I had to stand up to suck in some air, and I watched him come. Only at that moment did I realize that he was short, that his body was much smaller than mine. When he reached my side, he looked at me for a moment and then handed me another berry he had in his hand. This time, the fruit was green and warm. I took it, but didn't want to eat it.

"Green fruits give me a stomachache," I said, unsure of what else to do.

He smiled, and the whole world lit up with that smile.

"But come on, I discovered something you'll like." I took him by the hand and led him to the ditch.

I had planned this for many nights. I'd lie down to sleep, close my eyes, and think about how to make friends with him. I had decided that it was best to show him that I also liked the stuff you could find in the ditch.

We didn't say anything to each other along the way. I just needed him to come with me to the place I'd been preparing, I squeezed his hand tight so he wouldn't escape. Soon I could feel him starting to sweat. When we reached the edge of the ditch, I didn't find what I expected. There were supposed to be some aquatic flowers—a species of lotus, the gardener had told me, that would surely thrive in that water. After breakfast that morning they'd been there, but now that I needed them, they didn't appear. Nervous and not letting go of his hand, I dragged David a few more steps, checking the edge of the water that ran slowly and calmly. They were not there.

I turned back without giving his hand a chance to break free, and then I found them. With relief I checked that all my preparations had not been in vain. We crouched down, and I pointed at the yellow flowers.

"They're like lily pads. In the Amazon there are some so big you can sit on them without sinking."

He looked me in the eye and then shot me, smiling. Of course, playing along, I fell on my back, dropping his hand, looking up at the gray clouds that had begun to cover the sun.

"They're pretty," he said finally.

"I wanted to show them to you. They're free-floating flowers." I sat up and tried to remember everything I had prepared to interest him in me. "They don't stick to anything. They stick their roots in the water and the water can take them anywhere."

He had crouched down, bringing his nose close to the edge to examine them.

"It seems that these flowers have more——" His hand shot out into the water. The slapping splash made me fall backward.

"What is it?" I asked, getting up and brushing the dirt off my butt.

He opened his hand and showed me a tadpole squirming in his palm. Leaning forward, I saw that under the green leaves of the yellow lotuses there was a pretty big school of tadpoles. I figured they liked the shade the leaves made underwater. They began to scuttle out of sight, so I also reached out to grab one. Incredibly, when I pulled my hand out of the water, a small slimy creature was wriggling between my fingers. I moved it to the palm of my hand and showed it to my friend, who frowned. There was something he didn't like.

"Should we leave it in the water?" I asked. He nodded.

I did as we'd agreed with mine and waited for him to do the same, so we could take the next step in our eventual friendship. But instead he tossed the tadpole into his mouth, swallowed it in a single gulp, and ran off toward the building, leaving me alone. I thought about that slimy thing sliding down my throat.

That day I wasn't able to learn anything else about him.

I ended up sick, vomiting up everything I'd eaten the last few days.

11

"I DON'T KNOW, don't know, don't know, don't know," Manuela repeated, looking down at the floor. Maria and Hector watched her, waiting for a confession.

"I won't give you back your blankie," Maria threatened, Manuela's raggedy blanket in her hand.

Manuela reached up and jumped, trying to grab it, but her forehead slapped against Maria's hand, which glued her firmly to the ground.

"Give it to me!" the little one whined.

"Not until you tell me what happened to Robert!" said Maria.

Hector put his hands on his hips and glared at Manuela as if he could pull things out of her head with his eyes.

"He said he was leaving," she confessed, jumping again to try to grab her blanket.

"And?" Maria prompted, holding the blanket higher.

"That he was going to live on the streets because you guys are mean," Manuela sobbed, slumping to the floor. Next to her rose a little mountain of eucalyptus seeds she had been playing with.

"And David?"

"He went with Doña Yeni, to help her with the shopping," Manuela blurted through tears, knocking over the eucalyptus seeds in frustration.

"Stop carrying this thing around, Manuela. You're too big for baby stuff," said Maria, throwing the blanket over her head. Manuela seized it like a prize and immediately put it in her mouth.

"Quit sucking on it!" Maria demanded, grabbing a corner and yanking it from her lips.

"Leave me alone! Leave me alone! Leave me alone!" screamed Manuela, threatening to throw the seeds at her. "You're not my bosses. That's why Robert left! You're meanies!"

Maria and Hector looked at each other, at a loss.

"Shh, shhh," said Hector, hugging the little girl and staring again at Maria. "Don't be like that. It's just that we have to stick together."

"Why?" sobbed Manuela, leaning against her brother's shoulder.

"Because we're a family."

Maria turned her back on them and leaned her elbows on the windowsill, looking out at the courtyard. She saw David entering, his face hidden by the huge grocery bag he carried on his shoulder. He stumbled along under the weight. Doña Yeni, behind him, dragged some sacks that cleared a path behind her through the scattered leaves and seeds.

"Why hasn't Doña Yeni paid rent?" asked Maria.

Hector let go of his little sister, who kept squeezing herself tightly against him anyway, and sighed.

"Because Robert told her to give us food instead of rent."

"And she washes our clothes," Manuela added.

Maria clenched her teeth and left the room. Hector got up and ran after her, stopping her in the courtyard.

"Where are you going?"

"To look for Robert, where else?"

"I'll go with you," said Hector, and they headed out together.

Manuela, standing in the doorway of their room, saw them leave and then watched David's awkward attempts to drag the bag up the stairs.

"I've got it," Doña Yeni grunted, pushing him aside and picking up the bag. "Thanks. Oh, and take this for the girl."

She handed him two bananas. David stood there several moments, trying to catch his breath, until Manuela walked over, dragging her blanket. She pulled his pant leg out of his boot and reached out her hand to receive her share.

※※※※

AFTER SEVERAL HOURS, they sat down on one of the park benches. They did not notice the intense orange that seemed to set fire to the few clouds above and to draw from the walls and abandoned quarries another halo that transformed that red and yellow world—all brick and sand, motley houses perched on mined-out hills without a hint of green—into a slick and vibrant surface poised to become pure color, to abandon the shapes that defined it and dissolve completely into a sea of red, with no borders the eye could discern. But, on the other hand, the two knew that, after the intense afternoon sun, the clear sky was sign of a frigid night to come. They were silent for a moment until the cold made Maria's thin body shiver.

"What do we do now?" she asked, hugging herself to keep warm.

"I don't know," said Hector.

"We can't let him sleep on the street. He's only ten years old."

"But we've already looked everywhere," Hector groaned. "He probably left the neighborhood."

They sat there in silence for another moment until Maria couldn't stand the cold anymore and decided to get up.

"Let's go home. He might be back already."

But they didn't find Robert at home, either. Instead, Manuela and David were asleep, hugging each other in bed. Hector watched as Maria put her hair up and, moving the way their mother had, started preparing dinner.

"Maria," Hector said very softly, so the younger children wouldn't wake up.

"Yes?" Maria answered, unconcerned about the noise she was making with the pots and pans.

"I think we're doing okay . . . don't you?"

Maria stopped chopping tomatoes. She rubbed her eyes with the back of the hand that held the knife, as if drying an invisible tear. "I don't know. Maybe."

"If Julio gets me the job . . ." Hector said and saw how Manuela's huge eyes opened up under her pink blanket, locked on him, glowing with hope. Walking over, he stroked the little one's tangled hair and sighed.

"If only Mom were here."

Maria slammed the knife against the cutting board, sending chopped tomato flying.

"Our mother is dead!" She turned toward them, her angry voice reverberating through the room.

David woke up. Eyes blurred by a fog of sleep, he tried to understand what was happening.

"I miss her," Manuela whispered. "And Dad too."

"Dad's coming back," Maria said fiercely. "I just know it. And stop your whining! It makes everyone sad!"

She stamped her foot at Hector, who was groaning quietly beside Manuela. Now it was the little girl who stroked his head with her chubby hand, consoling him.

"When?" asked David.

"Soon," Maria replied, and began to pick up pieces of tomato from the floor.

꧄

SUNDAYS WERE THE ONLY DAYS when Doña Yeni did not wake them early, so when she knocked on the door of the room, the children were still asleep. The first to jump up was Maria, who ran to open the door. In burst the intense light of morning that had snuck through the courtyard toward their room. Eucalyptus air filled her lungs.

"What's the matter?" Maria asked as she opened and found their boarder standing in front of her.

"They're asking for Hector at the front door," replied Doña Yeni.

Maria was turning to call him when the woman stopped her.

"I mean, it might be better if you told him not to talk to that boy anymore. He could end up going down a bad path," she said.

Maria just shrugged and went back in to wake her brother.

※※※

"**WHERE?**" **ASKED HECTOR**, trying to shake sleep from his head as he stood by the curb.

"I'll take you. Come on, get on the bike. He's down there with the huffers," Julio replied.

"Thank you," said Hector.

"No problem. That's what friends are for." Julio smiled. Hector nodded.

He walked back to the room to put on his shoes.

"They found Robert! I'm going to get him," he announced to his siblings.

"I'm coming with," said Maria, bouncing up like a spring.

"No. I'm going with Julio, on his motorcycle. Wait here. If I bring him back, we can go to the park and eat ice cream," he said, and the little ones cheered.

12

I COULDN'T LOOK HIM IN the eyes again. Every time we crossed paths, I remembered his frown, his hand rising toward his mouth, and I imagined what he must have felt when he swallowed the tadpole he'd just plucked the water. My stomach turned at all the details I could think of, the slippery but solid little body slipping through his teeth, its tail waggling in his throat, its frantic twisting and turning as it reached his stomach, the taste of puddles and rotting reeds, and then the burps that later on would remind him a tadpole was in his belly.

I couldn't even think about him. Every time my memory brought his face to my mind, which happened several times a day—in class, at recess, in the bathroom, in the cafeteria—I had to get him out of my head as soon as possible, terrified at what disgust might make me do. I tried not to run into him. When there was no way to avoid crossing paths, I did my best not to look at him. It wasn't that I didn't like him anymore; it was the idea of throwing up everything I had eaten again that I didn't like. So, since I knew it was a problem with my gut and that I still wanted to be his friend, instead of looking at him, letting him kill me, and then having to run to the nearest bathroom to vomit, I figured out ways to leave some of my food next to him without his noticing. It was dumb. Maybe he never realized that the extra portions came from me. I don't even know if he ate what I left, but since he was always hungry I figured he did. My fantasy was that the little closeness we had achieved was kept alive.

However, after a few days, I began to need someone to shoot me from a distance. So I decided to try out a trick. I began preparing even before opening my eyes in the morning. I remembered the feeling of a cool, sweet liquid running down my throat and combined it mentally with David's face. In bed, it worked. At least I could think of him without the sensation of a tadpole wriggling in my throat. I tried this a couple more times until in my mind I could imagine his face, his hair, his small and strong figure, his husky voice without my stomach doing somersaults to expel everything inside. Now I had to try the trick out in person.

That day it wasn't hard to find him. He was going up the stairs of the building, carrying a giant black bag. I was on the top landing so that I could look at him for a few seconds and force my mind to put his image together with the feeling of swallowing a bit of strawberry ice cream. My mouth was watering by the time he finally saw me, put the black bag aside, pointed at me, and killed me. I fell dead slowly while still looking at him and wondering if one day we could actually eat ice cream together.

13

SHE LET HER HAIR DOWN, which she had been wearing in a bun lately, and shook her head. She looked down at her reflection in the display case. She could barely make out her features in the dark image she saw. She took a breath and rapped the glass with her knuckles.

"Doña Carmen!" she shouted. "Doña Carmen, it's me, Maria!"

She waited a second, and soon her attention was drawn toward the sound of someone moving toward her.

"Oh, dear girl . . ." the woman coming from the back

of the store complained. "You really are exactly like your father."

Maria smiled and lowered her eyes.

"Do you want something?" Carmen asked. "An agua-panela? A soda?"

"A soda would be great, Doña Carmen, thanks," Maria replied, watching as the woman's ample body moved slowly, retrieving a bottle and popping its cap.

"Here you go," she said, handing it to the girl.

Maria took a sip.

"Have you heard anything?"

"It's still not a sure thing," said the woman, "but I think tomorrow they're going to get me the phone number of a man in the town where your dad is. I can leave a message for him."

Maria set the bottle on the counter.

"Seriously?"

The woman nodded with a restrained smile.

"Yes, my dear, it seems so."

"Thank you," Maria whispered.

"Like I say, it's not a sure thing, but it seems likely. Still, don't get too excited. I don't want tears in those pretty eyes, if something goes wrong." She brushed a heavy, calloused hand across Maria's cheek.

Maria nodded and contained the tears Carmen had seen pooling.

"Incredible, girl. How old are you?"

"Twelve," Maria replied, looking down.

The woman shook her head.

"And the others? How are they? All right?"

〜〜〜〜〜

"AND YOU'VE BEEN left in charge?" asked the teacher.

"Yes," Hector answered without letting go of his sister's hand.

"What did you say your name is, child?"

"Manuela," the little girl replied, smiling.

"How old are you?" asked the teacher, beginning to fill out a form.

"Five," Manuela said.

"And why hasn't she come to school before?" asked the woman snidely.

"We couldn't . . ." Hector said quietly.

"But you're a minor! You cannot take care of another minor!"

"Please!" Hector pleaded. "It's just until my dad comes back."

The woman lifted her eyes, as if instead of a ceiling, she

might find the Most High who inspired her. She sighed, dropped her pen on the table loudly, and got up.

"I have to go check. I don't know if you can register her yourself."

Manuela looked at her brother.

"Are you hot?" she asked.

"No," he grunted, wiping his forehead with his shirt sleeve.

"Hector," Manuela whispered, "if they let me come to school, I won't suck my blankie no more, okay?"

Hector nodded and wiped more sweat from his forehead. They were silent for a moment, holding hands, until the teacher returned. She was smiling.

"We're in luck. There's a spot available," she said, plopping back into her seat at the table. "The girl can stay, and everything's copacetic because her brothers are enrolled already. But you have to pay the full tuition."

Hector's eyes widened.

"How much?"

"Thirty-five thousand pesos," said the woman, who was jotting something into the form.

Hector reached into his pocket and took out two twenty-thousand-peso bills. Enough for a week's worth of food.

"Can't we do it for less? This is all we have," he said, referring to the bills.

"No, boy. You have to pay in full or wait until next year to see if there's another slot. I mean, we're lucky, because before . . ."

Manuela stared up at the woman, who was waiting impatiently, and then reached for her brother's hand.

"Do I get lunch?" she asked.

"Yes. Lunch and a snack," the woman answered, smiling at her.

Hector sighed and handed over the crumpled bills. After pocketing the change, he ran his hand over Manuela's head. She looked up at him with a radiant grin.

"Thank you," said Hector.

"Come with me," the woman said, gesturing at the little girl.

Manuela released her brother's hand, handed him her pink blanket, and followed the woman into the school.

14

I DID IT AS IT POPPED INTO MY HEAD, almost without thinking I mean. As soon as I saw the music teacher, I ran to his side and asked him if I could take a friend to class. The music teacher, who's a really great guy, smiled and asked me:

"Does he know how to sing?"

I was silent for a moment wondering if I should lie or not. I decided not to. I wanted David to be with me in my favorite class.

"I don't know."

"Can he play an instrument?"

"I don't know that either, sir, but he loves music!" I lied then, but kept myself under control after and didn't say another word. When you start telling a lie, sometimes there's no way to stop. Of course, I had never said a word to David about music class. Just . . . I liked the class a lot and figured he might like it too. Plus it was a chance to spend more time with him.

"All right," said the teacher, clearly not believing me much, "tell him to come the next time we meet."

"Thank you, sir!" I said, bouncing with excitement. He shook his head, grinning.

Now my problem was getting close to David again. Then I had to convince him that going to music class was super cool, the absolute best.

Only then did I realize I was in over my head. The boy didn't even talk to me; he just shot me. As soon as I tried to have another conversation, he'd still run away. All my joy at the music teacher saying yes disappeared in a flash when I thought of how hard this was going to be.

It was lunchtime and, though I wasn't hungry, I stood in line waiting my turn. It moved so slow and I got very bored. I was just about to leave when a ruckus broke out behind me.

There he was, inside the cafeteria. A teacher held him,

pinning his arms and lifting him. He squirmed and kicked, fighting to get free. In front of them, one of the bigger kids was wiping his bloody nose. A younger girl was giving eager explanations to the teacher, who struggled not to lose his grip on David. The bigger kid looked at the floor, all embarrassed.

It was pretty easy to guess what had happened. I elbowed my way past a bunch of onlookers and got inside.

"He was defending me," I heard the girl say as the teacher dragged David to the back of the cafeteria.

"And you wait for me here until I come back, do you understand?" the teacher snapped at the bigger kid, still bleeding. "And the rest of you? Back in line, unless you want us to cancel lunch. Come over here, you."

He jerked his head at the girl, who followed him. I was right on her heels.

"So he defended you?" the teacher asked, after he'd managed to get them both to sit at a table. David was breathing heavy and wouldn't take his eyes off the bigger kid behind them.

"Yes, sir. That other boy pulled my hair. He yanked so hard he tore a chunk out!" the girl whined, pointing to the bigger kid and touching her messy hair. The teacher got closer and checked her head.

"Why?" he asked.

"I think it's because of him," she confessed, embarrassed, pointing at David.

"What do you mean?" the teacher asked.

"The other kid wanted to prove to everyone that he's not immortal."

"And that's why he hurt you?"

"Yes, so this one would see him hurting me and defend me. At first he did nothing, but when that kid said 'Look, Immortal Boy, what're you going to do about this?' he went crazy and busted his nose."

"Well, what's your name?" asked the teacher.

"David," the girl answered at last, breaking the silence. The boy looked at her for the first time.

"And why did you fight him?"

David shrugged without saying a word.

"You have to control yourself. I don't mean that it's not right to defend the little ones, but you have to be careful because it can end badly." David looked at the ceiling and then at the table.

"Do you go to the psychologist?" continued the teacher, while behind us, kids were pushing their way back into the lunch line.

David nodded without opening his mouth.

"Look, you were lucky this time, but if you go up against

a group of boys, you could get hurt. You have to find a way to be calm."

"Maybe he could try music class?" I cut in, and the three suddenly realized I had been by their side since they arrived at the table.

"And who are you?" asked the teacher.

"A friend of David's," I said with a smile.

"Get moving. This has nothing to do with you." The teacher shooed me away with his hand.

"I'm going to go to music class," David announced. We all fell silent at the low rasp of his voice. A new scuffle started in the lunch line, and the bigger kid had disappeared from our sight. The teacher got up, looked at David, the girl, and me, and decided that it was better to go stop another fight from breaking out. Apparently, we weren't a problem anymore.

"Thank you," the girl said when we were alone. David nodded.

"Are you really going to music class?" I asked him, thinking that he might not have heard right with all the noise in the cafeteria.

"Yeah, when is it?" he replied, grinning at me, and again it was like he lit up the whole world. "I want to go outside. Did you already have lunch?"

David completely ignored the other girl, who stared at us, intrigued.

"Yes," I lied. "Come on, I'll go with you."

We walked away, leaving the girl he'd defended without a word, as she waved goodbye.

15

MARIA RAN TO THE DARK display case and without waiting for Doña Carmen to emerge, slipped into the back of the house. She found the large, slow woman in front of the laundry room.

"Afternoon, Doña Carmen," said Maria. "Did you get it?"

The woman turned calmly with no change in expression. She began taking steps toward the storefront without responding.

"Did you get it? Did you get it?" Maria insisted at her side.

"I'm going, I'm going; just give me a moment. It's in here somewhere," the woman said lazily as she rifled through papers in a huge drawer. "Here it is."

She withdrew a slip of paper with a number jotted on one side.

"Should we call?" asked Maria excitedly. "Do you think maybe I can talk to him?"

"One moment, one moment," the woman insisted, overwhelmed. "Hold on, I'll put on my glasses."

She dropped heavily onto a wooden bench, clumsily setting the glasses on her nose. Because of how she squinted and grimaced, Maria guessed she actually saw better without glasses than with them, but she waited patiently for Carmen to confirm that the number she wanted was actually written on the card. When the woman was satisfied, she picked up the phone and dialed.

"I can only allow you one call, and a short one at that," she said, handing Maria the telephone receiver. "Give your daddy your message quick and hang up, okay?"

Maria nodded and, holding the phone with both hands against her ear, listened to the tinny ring, her eyes bright with excitement.

/////

"WHAT ARE WE going to eat?" asked David, rubbing at his runny nose. Beside him, Manuela, a finger between her teeth, awaited the answer.

"Soup," Maria replied with an annoyed grunt. "And instead of asking, why don't you go and ask Doña Yeni for more potatoes?"

"She said she wouldn't give no more," Manuela replied.

"Supposedly we eat more than the whole neighborhood," David added.

"That old bitch," Robert spat. "Let *me* go ask her."

"Yeah, you go. It was your idea not to charge her rent."

Robert left the notebook on which he was scribbling some homework, went out to the courtyard, and ran up the stairs. David and Manuela looked out the window, waiting. When nothing happened, they ducked back under the table to continue playing.

"And neither of you has any homework?" demanded Maria, watching the water start to boil in the pot.

"Nope!" they both replied, covering their mouths so they wouldn't laugh, making signs for the other to keep the secret.

"Oh, you'll see what happens. Won't be me they refuse to give a snack to."

Manuela and David looked at each other and climbed out to get their backpacks.

"Maria," Manuela said, once she had her notebook on her lap, "if I don't wear a uniform, they won't let me in."

"The first thing you need to do is take a bath, little piggy," Maria muttered, looking her over. "Then later we can take in one of mine so it fits you."

"Doña Yeni can help. She knows how to sew," David said.

At that moment the door of the room opened, and Hector stumbled in, smelling like gasoline. He threw himself onto the bed and groaned.

"What happened?" asked Manuela.

"I fell off Julio's motorcycle!" he answered, wincing with the pain.

Maria rolled her eyes and smirked. "Oh, poor baby! He fell!"

"Look, if I don't learn to ride, Julio can't help me get a job."

"Ah, he's finally going to give you one?" asked Maria.

"If I learn to ride. If I stop falling off. He told me it was a test to see how it goes."

"How what goes?"

"Stuff!" Hector replied. "Me. How I manage, you know."

Manuela and David watched them argue as if they were two adults.

"And how many times did you fall?"

"Twice. Bashed myself pretty hard." Hector stood up to show his sister a scraped leg.

"Boom. Straightened her out. Here they are!" Robert announced smugly as he pushed through the door with a bag of potatoes in his arms. "Damn! You got busted up. Playing football?" He jerked his head toward his older brother's leg.

"No, on Julio's motorcycle."

"He's teaching you how to ride?"

"Yup."

Hector and Robert looked at each other.

"What's wrong with you weirdos?" asked Maria impatiently.

"Nothing," said Hector. "Here, I was able to scrape this together."

He handed Maria a wad of bills.

16

THINGS NEVER HAPPEN the way I imagine. Last night I kept staring into the darkness above me and listening to the slow and steady breathing of my roommates, until the moon filled the entire room with a blue glow. Not good. I've never been able to sleep when the lights are on. The darker the room, the better I sleep.

In Chía, the town where this place is, the moon rises so huge when it's full you almost think it'll fall out of the sky, right smack onto the earth, just like in that old story. And the light it casts is just as huge. Trust me. Even with the curtains tightly closed, my back turned, my face hidden under the pillow or blankets, the moonlight slips through to the center of my forehead and won't let me sleep.

And that's what happened that night.

So I started to think. There were two things that bugged me. The first was what I was going to say to the psychologist at our next appointment. There was so much to share. I figured that if she played the music of that man again, I'd end up telling her all about my mother and my father. I wouldn't mind crying. I would let all the tears I had saved pour out and mix with that music that seemed to come from the same sad place. I would tell her that my father was a political prisoner and was in a penitentiary on the coast. While we were still together, my mother and I had been able to go see him twice. He had been getting skinnier, his hands shaking more and more. But ever since my mother was arrested for the same crime and they brought me to this place, I hadn't heard from him again.

I would share that when they told me I could not live with my family, I thought my life was going to end. I still hoped my mother would get out of prison very soon, like she had promised me. But I would also admit that now I was terrified of never seeing David again, and that I had never felt so close to someone who wasn't a family member. We had begun to spend much more time together thanks to music class. The truth is he was much better than me at drawing out the melody from the songs they taught us and playing it on basically any instrument. Instead of getting angry like I usually did when someone was better than me, I felt proud and happy that he was so good, that the teacher kept congratulating him every chance he got. Who knows, if the psychologist put on that beautiful music for him, maybe David could lift the notes out and play them on some instrument for everyone in class. I planned to share it all with the psychologist that afternoon.

The other thing that bugged me was that David had something to show me. That's what he had told me last time. My plan was to leave the psychologist's office and meet him to see what he wanted. But things don't always happen the way you imagine.

So, when it was time to get up, it felt like I had barely lain down to sleep and the blue light of the moon had left my body weak. I bathed slower than ever, I made my bed, and I dragged myself to the cafeteria for breakfast. Since they served us breakfast and dinner in the small dining room, there was no point in keeping an eye on the faces that passed. I wasn't going to see him there. Me and David, we only crossed paths at school, on the playground, by the ditch, and in the large dining room, at lunchtime. But there are things you do even if there's no point. You just can't help yourself.

I was finishing my café con leche—mostly warm milk—a little dizzy from glancing side to side so much, my eyes heavy and my body warm, when the person in charge of my group arrived and headed straight to my table.

"Nina, didn't you sleep?" she asked me as she sat down by my side and checked my face.

"The moon didn't let me," I replied, and she laughed as if we were both in on a white lie.

"Go change. Put on normal clothes," she said. My eyes snapped open. I was intrigued and awake. "You have a visit with your mother at noon."

"Do I . . . not go to class?"

"Only the first two," she replied. "Someone will pick you up at the secretary's office at twelve. What classes do you have?"

"I have an appointment with the psychologist." I must have been making a strange face because the woman asked me:

"Aren't you happy? You get to see your mom . . ." She looked at me like I was a weirdo.

"Can I take my flute?" I asked. I had learned a song and wanted my mom to hear it.

"Sure!" The woman smiled at me. "But hurry!"

I was so happy, imagining my mother's hand on my

cheek. I left without finishing the milky coffee and ran out to put on my prettiest clothes, to pick up the drawings I'd made, the stories I'd written.

The woman smiled again, to herself, and examined what was left on my plate.

DAD IS COMING BACK," she said, and Hector found himself oddly surprised at the amount of hair his sister Maria had.

Manuela began to jump on the bed, making it creak.

"When?" asked Robert.

"He sent a message for us to wait for him together. He'll be back soon."

"Didn't he say when?" asked David.

Maria shook her head.

"Well, that's the same thing he said when he left!" Robert protested.

"Yes. But this time he sent us a message that we should behave well and wait for him together."

"Did you talk to him?" Robert insisted.

"No. I said he sent a message for us to wait for him together," Maria repeated, annoyed.

"Together," Hector said to Robert. "You heard that, yeah?"

"Who did he send a message with?" David asked, while Manuela kept jumping beside him on the bed, making him tremble.

"With Doña Carmen's friend," said Maria, who had enough of her brothers' interrogations.

"The old gossiping woman with the store in her house?" asked Robert.

"She doesn't gossip! Besides, we've had dinner more than one night with food she's given us, just so you know!"

"She's a pain in the ass!" Robert insisted. "The other night—"

"That's enough!" Maria stopped him. "Aren't you guys happy that Dad is coming back?"

"I am," Manuela babbled, still jumping. "He'll see that I don't suck on my blankie no more, right, Hector? And I don't sleep in the drawer no more, neither!"

As she finished, she made a final jump and then fell on

David, who groaned beneath his little sister's flailing legs.

"Me too," said Hector.

"And now you can go back to school," said Maria. "They keep asking when you'll be in class again."

"Not sure I'm going back to school," Hector muttered, sitting down next to David, who had recovered from the hit and was now carefully watching Manuela as she started jumping again beside him.

Maria glared at Hector as if she wanted to burn through him with her eyes.

"What do you mean you're not sure? What else are you going to do? Stock groceries at Corabastos? Do you think that's what Mom wanted for you?"

Everyone fell silent and looked at her.

HECTOR TOOK THE CURVE, tilting his body to the same side, and twisted his wrist back, accelerating. The engine hummed, and they passed between the idling buses, making obscene gestures to the drivers waiting to be dispatched to their routes. He slowed down a bit and pointed the motorcycle toward an abandoned lot. As he popped up onto the median, a truck crossed in front of him, coming slowly down from the highest part of the borough, and Hector shot toward the grass. He opened the throttle and held on tightly to the handlebars to withstand the sudden acceleration. Then he braked, dropping gears and making the rear tire spin a serpentine on the grass.

When they came to a full stop, he gunned the engine twice more and turned to his companion.

"What'd you think?" he asked, his cheeks chafed by the cold wind.

"Well, little bro, you've learned. Time for the next step," said Julio, who seemed younger sitting behind him on the bike. He jumped off and gestured for Hector to turn off the engine. Hector obeyed, popped the kickstand down, and lowered the motorcycle onto it. He got off, his legs feeling like he'd forgotten them for a long time, and took two wobbly steps toward Julio, who pointed to a huge cherry tree in the pasture.

"See that tree?" he asked.

"Sure," Hector said, thinking maybe it was a test of his eyesight.

"Good. Then pop a cap in it," said Julio, and pulled a revolver from his waistband. He pointed at the tree and let Hector watch him.

"Boom!" he shouted, amused to see the younger boy jump. "Now you got to learn to use it."

He set the revolver in Hector's open hand.

"This thing? Why?" Hector asked, not daring to curl his fingers around the warm metal.

"Just in case, kid. You never know what might happen. You gotta be ready, no?"

Hector shrugged, not knowing what to answer.

"What, you chickenshit or something?" Julio asked, sizing him up with a cold stare.

Hector held the gun in his palm, never taking his eyes off it.

"Look at it, fall in love with it. I'll leave you two alone so you can get to know each other. Just don't you lose it, eh?" Julio warned, hopping on the motorcycle and starting it with a kick.

The engine gave a high-pitched hum. He shifted into first and sped away, doing a wheelie. Then he braked, dropping the front wheel to the ground, and returned to the younger boy's side.

"Oh, and here. For expenses." Julio laughed, throwing a wad of bills at Hector. "If you run out of bullets, come look for me. Be ready for me to call you. And hey, don't be shooting nothing that moves. Not yet, you hear?"

He cackled loudly and rode off.

Hector stood there for a while, the metal object in his open hand, till he felt his fingers slowly curl around the pistol grip.

THE MIDDAY SUN pierced their skulls and bored into their brains, liquefying them and making the principal's endless stream of words seem like threads of melted gum.

When she finished her speech and announced that the school year was over, the students all loosed shouts. Summer vacation!

David was the first of the siblings to run out the school gate and stand next to the ice cream man, waiting for the others.

"Want a popsicle?" asked the man, letting the boy take a peek at the variety of ice cream in the cart.

David shook his head.

"You can pay me later," the man insisted.

"But it's the last day of school," David pointed out.

"The last day?" the man repeated, worried. "You kids don't come back tomorrow?"

David shook his head again.

"I'll pay you back?" asked David.

"Well, all right. Pay me the first day of school next year then."

David smiled excitedly and leaned forward to choose.

"Give me some!" said Robert, arriving a few minutes later to discover his younger brother enjoying a popsicle.

"Nope. It's mine. He said I could pay him back." David jerked his head at the ice cream man, who had moved his cart a few steps away to draw more customers. Then the boy continued to nibble on his treat.

"He's a freaking pig," Robert said when Maria arrived, holding Manuela by the hand. "Doesn't want to share."

"Why should I? I'm the one who got the ice cream. I can eat it all by myself."

"Imagine if we all acted like that," Maria said, shrugging. "None of us would eat at home."

Manuela approached her brother and took his free hand.

"Don't bother him, he's hungry," she announced fiercely.

David looked down at his little sister. She had confirmed what he'd always known: she was the sweetest girl in the world.

"Take it," he said, offering her the popsicle.

The girl took it, smiling, and got ready to give it a lick.

"Stingy brat!" Robert snarled. "Just you wait and see. You're going to get *so* hungry without school food, asshole."

Maria gave her brother a withering look and pushed him ahead.

"Come on," she ordered. "Let's go home!"

18

HE TOOK ME BY THE HAND and led me silently through the orchard to his favorite place. I had no clue what he was going to show me. My floating flowers had died days ago. Apparently, they didn't like the cold nights on the plains. I let myself get swept away without asking him anything, like he was guiding me with my eyes closed to a surprise cake baked for my birthday.

"It's over here," he said as we reached the ditch, like I hadn't known his special spot for ages.

"Look," he said at last, stopping under one of the

branches of the willow that drooped into the water. He pulled out a bucket. I looked down into it and saw there were a ton of tadpoles wriggling and squirming frantically against each other. One of them had begun its metamorphosis and now had a tiny pair of legs near its long tail. David looked at it carefully for a long time. I didn't dare say a thing. I focused on the pollywogs, trying to understand his fascination with these nasty, slimy baby frogs. David reached in and carefully took the tadpole with legs between his fingers. I feared the worst. I knew I couldn't handle watching him swallow another tadpole in front of me, especially one that already had legs, so I closed my eyes.

"Open your eyes," he said. He was pointing at the tadpole with legs, escaping into the slimy darkness of the mud. "It took off. It'll become a frog."

I looked at him, hoping he would finally reveal his secret.

"All of them will become frogs, won't they?" I asked.

"No. Not all of them. These are mine," he said with a strange glint in his eyes. "These aren't going to become frogs. This is my tadpole farm."

I nodded. I figured he was in the middle of something that not even he completely understood, so I smiled at him, trying to make things less awkward. He hid the bucket again under the camouflage of the willow branches, making sure that the ditch water didn't reach the lip and spill inside.

"They're *my* tadpoles," he insisted, looking at me expectantly.

What could I say? Suddenly I remembered that everyone called him the Immortal Boy.

"I shouldn't have shown them to you," he said after a moment, pushing me so I fell to the ground. "You don't understand either."

I stood up, angry.

"How will I understand if you don't explain to me?" I demanded, being careful not to mention his immortality at all.

But it was too late. He was walking away, his only answer, again, the sight of his back swaying from side to side.

19

ALTHOUGH THEY WERE not as chubby any-more and had lost those dimples in the knuckles he liked so much, David insisted on holding his sister's hands in his own. Manuela looked at him with glassy eyes and cracked lips. They were alone in the room and he didn't know what else to do to calm the girl's trembling.

"More water?" he asked, offering her the cup he held in his free hand.

Manuela shook her head and her breathing became agitated. A whistling sound came from her chest with every inhalation.

"Don't wheeze, Manue," David begged.

"I can't stop," the girl replied with a shudder.

David closed his eyes, and everything was submerged in deep silence, except for the desperate wheeze of the girl's chest. After listening for a while, David thought that maybe a little air would do her some good, so he let go of her hands and opened the door. Indeed, a fresh breeze slipped through the open space and reached his little sister.

"David," she said, opening her eyes, "I want panela."

David walked over to the kitchen table and checked everywhere. Nothing.

"Let's wait for Maria to come home," David replied. "She'll bring food."

Manuela closed her eyes again and rested, breathing more calmly. Her chest stopped wheezing, and David congratulated himself on having thought of opening the door.

Sitting down next to his sister, he began counting the fingers on her hands, again and again.

⁂

"WHAT'S GOING ON?" asked Hector, rubbing his eyes and trying to make something out in the darkness.

"She's burning up," answered Maria.

Hector got up and went to the little kids' bed. There were his brothers: Robert asleep with his butt in the air and his cheek against the pillow, and on the other side, David, hugging Manuela close. He had his eyes open and was looking at her carefully as if afraid of missing something.

"Come over to this bed," said Hector.

David shook his head.

"Come on, man," the older boy insisted, "that way you'll let her sleep, and you can sleep too."

"What's the matter with her?" asked David. He obeyed. "Is she going to die?"

The darkness kept him from seeing the fierceness in his older sister's eyes.

"Why do you say things like that?" Maria demanded as he settled into the big kids' bed.

"Is she real sick? She's wheezing just like Mom did," David insisted. "Before she died."

Hector rubbed his head.

"Tomorrow she'll be fine," the older boy assured him. "Let's not talk about it now."

David looked up, trying to figure out if he was telling the truth or just calming him down. He decided it was true and closed his eyes.

※※※

"SHE'S BEEN CRYING for three hours," Maria complained. She had pulled her hair into a bun, as was her new habit, and was pacing next to the bed where Manuela kept on incessantly. David and Robert stared at their desperate sister from the doorway.

"Manuela," said Robert, "what's wrong with you?"

But like every other time he'd asked, there was no response but the slow, long crying that drifted from the lungs of the little girl as if it were her very breath.

⁄⁄⁄⁄⁄

DAVID WALKED OUT, leaving the door open. In the courtyard the smell of eucalyptus was almost overpowering. Someone was probably cutting them down or burning them nearby. He went up the stairs and knocked on Doña Yeni's door. No sounds came from inside. David tried again and again. After the third time, the woman peeked through the door without opening it all the way.

"What do you want?" she asked, her eyes swollen.

"Manuela is still sick," said the boy, not knowing how to broach the issue. "She just wants some panela . . ."

The woman softly cursed, mumbling something David couldn't quite make out, and went back into her room. She immediately emerged again, a bag in her hand.

She was still muttering profanities as she headed down the stairs, but David didn't care. He followed her, excited. Their neighbor had once cured him of a stomachache.

"Poor girl," Doña Yeni whispered, after looking at Manuela for a moment.

"What's happening to her?" asked David in a rush.

"The same thing that's happening to all of you," said the woman with a sigh.

David didn't understand why she had to sigh so much instead of just telling him what was wrong.

"Well, what's happening to us?" asked David, feeling that he was going through motions that only mattered to her.

"When is your dad going to show up?" asked the woman, walking to the kitchen table and moving junk out of the way.

"Maria is the one who knows," David explained.

"And where is she?"

David just shrugged in response.

"Here's what we're going to do," the woman proposed as David nodded. "We'll wait for your brothers and sister to arrive, and I'll tell you all."

THE FOUR SPOONS scraped the remnants of soup from the bottom of the bowls. David's eager eyes checked his siblings' plates for any scraps. They had eaten everything. He sighed and stared at Doña Yeni. The woman had watched them eat in silence while giving Manuela slow spoonfuls. The girl slowly and reluctantly took in the warm soup. Much of the liquid dribbled down her chin. When they had finished, Doña Yeni took a breath, collected the dishes, and looked at Maria.

"Okay, so when is he coming?"

"Who?" asked Hector.

"Your dad, who else?" said the woman.

Maria took the dishes from her and went toward the door, heading outside to wash them.

"Wait a minute, Maria."

The girl stopped with her eyes down, as if sensing what was coming.

"Thanks for the soup, Doña Yeni," said Maria, avoiding the woman.

"Maria," Robert said.

"What do you want?" she asked, looking up and slamming the plates back down on the table. The sharp sound of ceramic on wood cracked through the room.

"When's Dad arriving? Did you really even talk to him?" Robert spat.

Manuela had fallen asleep in her chair and was about to fall over, but Maria rushed over to hold the girl up. Then she picked her up and carried her to bed. The little girl babbled a couple of syllables and curled up to keep sleeping.

"Maria?" said Doña Yeni.

David and Hector sat there, waiting.

"I don't know when he'll arrive! I have no idea. He just sent word that we're supposed to wait for him together," Maria replied, looking from person to person.

"Sure you didn't just . . . make up the whole thing, so you could boss us around?" demanded Robert, glancing at Doña Yeni for her approval.

"No," said Maria simply. She stared at them defiantly.

"Can't we just send him another message to see what he wants us to do?" asked Hector in a more conciliatory tone.

"I tried," Maria replied. "Doña Carmen couldn't track him down again . . ."

They regarded one another in silence until a new stream of senseless babble came from Manuela's cracked lips.

"Look, I don't know," Doña Yeni began, "but you kids can't go on like this."

Everyone stared at her.

"Like what?" asked Maria.

"Like *this*—starving to death!" Doña Yeni replied. Then she pointed at Manuela. "Do you want to know what's wrong with your little sister? Hunger. I don't give a damn what happens to you, but you ought to go to Social Services to see if they can set you up someplace where you'll at least have food to eat."

"Social Services?" Robert growled. "I am *not* going to Social Services."

"We can't let them separate us," said Hector. "Dad told me we shouldn't split up."

"When?" demanded Doña Yeni.

"Before he left."

Again everyone fell silent. Without a word, David lay down next to Manuela and hugged her tightly to him.

"We want to stay together," said Maria. "At Social Services they separate kids."

"But they give them food and clothes," said Doña Yeni. "And doctors! It's a sin this little girl is sick. If it was up to me, I would round you all up and take you there now."

"Don't tell them anything," Robert begged.

"I've almost got a job," Hector said. "They're going to call me in to work soon, and then we won't ask you for anything else except to help us take care of the house."

David, hugging Manuela, looked at Doña Yeni's face and saw that slight sneer on her lips, the same expression she made when he dropped something he was helping her carry.

"You'll see soon enough," Doña Yeni concluded. "But I'm going to spend Christmas and New Year's with family, and you all will be alone. I won't be able to help you with anything. What're you going to do?"

"Our dad is coming back," Maria said.

"And I'm going to start working," Hector added.

"You'll see soon enough. Anyway, I'll leave you some food," she said, picking up the dirty dishes and heading for the door. "I pray to God it's enough. I can't spare too much, and, besides, I'll be away for nearly two months."

David buried his face next to his sister. From the pillow came the warmth of her breath.

"I pray to God it's enough," the woman repeated, heading outside with the dishes.

"That bitch," Robert growled when she was gone. "She's going to report us."

※※※

ALTHOUGH HE HAD only been on the street for two days, his face and hands were already blackened, as if all the filth of the city had smeared on his skin. He dropped the bag he'd been huffing and tried to stand. But his legs, made wobbly by the glue, would not support him, so he fell like a rag doll onto his sleeping friends. Nobody even flinched at the impact. Sprawled willy-nilly on top of them, he laughed at not being able to move his own body, and closed his eyes to sleep.

A hand shook him several times. It was Hector. He opened his eyes and realized that his brother was repeating his name and pulling him. Beside him was also Maria, her hair up in its usual bun. For the first time he saw that his sister looked a lot like his mother. He didn't like the idea and closed his eyes again.

"Don't you do this to me again, Robert," he heard one of them warn him.

They walked slowly, supporting his body between them. Up the streets that led to their house. When they stopped, he opened his eyes again and found they had reached the door. His body leaned heavily on his older sister. He felt the warmth of her breath on his face and liked it. He smiled and muttered something nice. The vulgar insult that his sister let fly cracked him like a whip, and he went completely limp in her arms.

"I'm going to see if I can find Julio," announced Hector, leaving Robert in Maria's arms. His sister scoffed.

"Yeah, and when was the last time you saw him?" She let her little brother drop to the ground. "Whatever, but I am *not* going to bathe him by myself, and he's too filthy to come inside."

Hector sighed, turned around, and walked away.

"Then just leave him on the steps until he wakes up."

~~~

"DID YOU FIND HIM?" asked Maria.

"No. They say he's not coming back to our neighborhood," Hector said with a shrug.

"What're we going to do?"

Hector grabbed his head with both hands, as if ready to yank his hair out. They were sitting on the porch steps, talking in hushed, almost secret tones.

"David's stopped talking," Maria told him.

"What do you mean?" asked Hector.

"Just what I said. He won't talk. Doesn't respond. He's been that way for about eight days. Not a word. He just sits next to Manuela and says nothing."

"I haven't noticed it," said Hector.

"How could you notice anything? You spend every day on the streets!"

"I've been looking for Julio," he shot back, trying to justify himself.

"Stop looking for him. He doesn't want to be found. And you're better off without him, Hector. That guy has a bad reputation."

"Well, he gave me a lot of money."

"And has he made you, uh, 'pay him back' yet?" asked Maria with a wicked grin.

"What? No. He's going to give me a job, I told you. Stop letting your twisted mind imagine sick stuff! No wonder everyone's scared of your face, you troll."

Maria sighed.

"Tomorrow's Christmas," she whispered instead. "I miss Mom, too."

She leaned against Hector's shoulder. He put his arms around her, and they sat that way in silence, looking up at the stars whose light had finally found its way to their courtyard. Their neighbors had cut down the huge eucalyptus trees that used to fill it with seeds.

"What will we eat tomorrow?" Maria wondered aloud.

Hector did not answer.

"Should we go to Social Services? I'm sure they'll take us in. And maybe, if we tell them to leave all five of us together . . ."

"No. Better off dead," Hector said, not taking his eyes off the sky. "I promised Dad I wouldn't let anything tear us apart."

20

I FIGURED THAT, since I'd stopped feeling the squirming of tadpole tails in my throat every time I saw David, perhaps I could also manage to swallow one myself. Maybe that was what he wanted to tell me, that we should eat tadpoles together. I didn't understand why it would be so important for him that I get one of those nasty slugs in my belly, but if that was what he really wanted, I had to come up with a way to do it.

The first thing was to try to find something that felt like a pollywog. Once my dad had taken me to eat oysters, and I had also thrown up. But, yeah, I wasn't getting any oysters in *this* place. Then an idea occurred to me. It was disgusting and I had to pray it wouldn't hurt me, but the result was good. I asked the kitchen to give me some little Andean potatoes.

"What do you want them for?" they asked me.

"For an experiment," I replied with a smile.

I knew that even if it was the absolute truth, the kitchen ladies weren't going to believe me anyway. And they didn't, but I guess they thought it would be hard for me to do any serious damage with them, so they gave me a bag of some round yellow potatoes. I washed them carefully, put them in a jar of water, and left them under my bed.

The process shouldn't have taken more than five days, but when I checked them, almost all of them were still hard. Then I did something *really* gross. But the idea wasn't mine. I got it from history class. The teacher told us that, to make the alcoholic drink called chicha, Indigenous people would spit into pots full of crushed corn. That's how they accelerated fermentation. And since that was what I wanted, I went ahead and spit into the jar where my potatoes were still nearly completely fresh. As much drool and mucus as I could hack up. It was mine anyway.

Then I waited two more days.

Things had to work out for me this time. The first step

was to prepare my stomach and my mind to swallow slimy, disgusting stuff.

The second step was finally talking to him. My mother had already been in jail for six months and we expected her to be released in less than four more. I focused every day, as hard as I could, on the idea that she'd be released within that period, that the days would pass quickly, that those months would be as light as a sigh. My mother getting released was the best thing that could happen in my life. But I also knew that when she left, I would have to leave this place and never see David again. That seemed to me the worst thing that could happen in my life.

My mother, the best in the world, had explained to me when I visited her that the minute she got out of prison, we would probably have to leave the country. She told me I should start saying goodbye to David.

"I can't," I told her frankly.

"It's for the best. If we could stay, that would be another story. But the safest thing for both of us is to be out of the country until your dad gets out."

"What if you adopt him?" I asked, not giving her a chance to think it through.

She smiled at me and pressed my head against her chest. When she sighed, I could see the small scar on her bare ear.

"How do you know he wants someone to adopt him?" she asked. "Not everyone wants to have a family."

"He does," I assured her.

Although I was lying, I imagined that David, like me, wanted to have a family. I would have been happy being part of his family.

In the end, my mother didn't say yes or no. But when things were like that with her, it sometimes meant yes. So now what I needed was to be able to swallow disgusting and slimy things to become his best friend, so I could talk with him and ask if he wanted my mom to adopt him when she got out of prison.

When I removed the lid from the jar of potatoes, the dorm room was filled with a smell so revolting my room-mates threw me out. Holding the jar in the middle of the cold corridor, I took what was left of one of the potatoes between my fingers. I thought again about strawberry ice cream, very intensely. I waited until I felt the cold against my teeth and the creamy goodness easing down my throat, its fresh sweetness. Then I put that slimy, stinky stuff as far back as possible on my tongue, and without even breathing, I swallowed it, just another soft piece of ice cream.

Differently than I had supposed, my stomach kept it all down. After a while I had swallowed every single rotten potato in the jar. I felt a little dizzy, but I figured it was from all the excitement and mental effort I had made to achieve my goal.

I washed the jar and went to sleep, happy I had learned to master my body.

The next day I couldn't move from the toilet, but the important thing had already happened:

I could swallow anything slimy and gross without vomiting on the spot.

21

HAT DAY MANUELA was the first to open her eyes. She woke up feeling good and ready to play, the first time in forever. But since everyone else was still asleep and she knew how angry Maria got if she was awakened early, Manuela instead stared at each of her siblings in turn. She realized, for example, that Robert's breathing was the shallowest of all, that Hector slept with an eye half-open, that Maria didn't close her mouth and always gripped the blanket in one hand, and that David breathed slow and steady. She stared at him without blinking until her gaze made him open his eyes.

"Want to go outside?" she asked in a whisper. "The sun's up."

She looked at him intensely, as if trying to get into his head. David blinked a few times to make sure he wasn't seeing things.

"Are you okay?" asked the boy once he got her in focus.

"Yes," Manuela smiled. "Will you show me?"

She kept grinning, showing her little baby teeth. David sat up, saw that the others were still asleep, and got out of bed. He took his sister's hand and led her to the courtyard.

"But there's nothing left, Manuela. Why would you even go in there?" he said, trying to dissuade her as soon as they were outside.

"You promised me that as soon as I was well, you would show me . . ." Manuela whined, and David shrugged in resignation. Though he was really happy his sister felt better, her insistence seemed pointless.

"Do you know how to do it?" asked David.

Without answering, Manuela went up to Doña Yeni's door and stood there for a second, as if expecting it to open.

"I don't want to keep eating paper," Manuela complained. Her voice was particularly serious, and David, still looking at his little sister, shook his head.

"Me neither. But there's nothing there anymore. I already told you."

Manuela shrugged defiantly and, like a small cat, climbed up the wall to the roof. David watched her, terrified but unable to close his eyes. The little girl walked along the edge of the roof, arms stretched out for balance, then slid down to hang for a tense second before getting a foothold on a windowsill. From that perch she looked down at David and made a strange gesture.

"Don't be scared. I know the way," she assured her big brother, pushing the window open and slipping into the absent woman's room.

A few seconds later, David saw her appear again, opening the door to let him in.

"Shh. If Maria catches us, she'll kill us," she said, imitating him, waggling a scolding finger. Then she smiled.

She pulled her brother into the kitchen. In the basket that served as a pantry and that David had carried so many times, there sat a rotten potato, which the two of them stared at.

"You see?" David said, yawning with boredom. "There's nothing else. We already took everything."

The girl continued to check the space for food, her hands clenched into little fists. Her breathing came faster and faster, her small body shaking with slight shudders, as if some tiny animal were biting her all over.

David looked distractedly at the room he already knew

by heart, until his eyes stopped on a photo tacked to the wall. It was Doña Yeni, chasing chickens in a pen.

"Who's that?" asked Manuela.

David didn't answer. His eyes were absorbed by the image. Doña Yeni's hand was about to grab a red hen that ran with wings outspread and eyes wide. Hair almost completely covered the woman's face, and on her wide-stretched lips there was a grin that seemed to be tasting the animal's flesh already. Next to the foot that was on the ground, another chicken was fleeing, calmer and safe. David swallowed and felt his sister's glazed stare.

"Chickens eat, right?" Manuela asked, and a shiver racked her body.

"All animals eat," David answered. A new glow brightened his eyes, staring into the void, unseeing, until another shudder shot through his sister, making him react at last.

"Come on, Manue. The cold's going to make you sick again."

꩜

THE PARK WAS empty and Hector sat on a bench in its center. From time to time he looked toward the four streets that led to the park, waiting for some familiar face to appear. After a while he got up and with determined steps, headed down one of them.

As he advanced, he saw the evening star appear in the dark blue sky. He remembered that if he was the first to see it, he could make a wish. He closed his eyes, clenched his fists, and silently—in front of the business where his steps had led him—wished with all his might that everything that was happening would finally end. Then he entered and walked up to the counter. Behind it, as always, stood the woman. She smiled at him.

"Hey there, buddy. Merry Christmas," she said. "When're you going to get a job?"

Hector looked down. He noticed that the tip of his sneakers had been ripped open by the growth of his toes. The wood of the counter glowed deeper than it ever had on his previous visits.

"You hungry?" asked the woman, still smiling.

"Yes," Hector whispered. "Has Julio come by?"

"You need to stop looking for him," the woman said.

"I got to give him something back," said Hector.

"That guy ain't coming back," she insisted, beginning to straighten things up behind the counter.

"Maybe I can leave it with you?" asked Hector, taking the revolver out of his pocket. "I don't want to carry this thing anymore. I mean, what if it curses my hand or something?"

The metal caught the eye of the woman. She opened

her mouth as if trying to say something she couldn't. Instead she just shook her head.

Hector, without saying a word, put the weapon away and lowered his eyes, embarrassed.

"Look, I don't take care of those things. That's between you two. Don't get me involved," she said, shaking her head a bit as if trying to dislodge the image of the gun stamped on her brain. Then she proposed, "Have some soup instead."

The woman ladled a steaming plate and moved to set it on one of the tables.

"Besides, Julio probably got his ass beat for acting like a big shit, pretending he was some tough punk from Ciudad Bolívar. You got to know how to eat your fill nice and quiet. Especially here, where everyone is trying to screw everyone else just to save themselves." She continued in a whisper. "But eat, kid. No worries. We'll settle up later. I'm not so heartless I can't spare a little bowl of soup."

Hector sat down and looked at the soup. He stirred it with the spoon, but did not dare to try it.

"What? Is it that bad?"

"No." Hector gave a weak smile. "It's that my brothers and sisters . . ."

"Jesus. Why don't you let each one go their own way?"

She looked at him as if she already knew the answer. "If you want, I can take you in. But just you."

Hector pushed away the bowl, swallowed heavily, and stood.

"I promised my dad . . ." he murmured softly.

"What's that?" The woman could not hear him.

"Thanks for the soup. But I can't . . ."

"Wait, you're just going to leave it sitting there?"

"Sorry. If Julio comes, tell him I've got to give this back to him." Hector touched his pocket where he had put the gun and took a few steps toward the door. "Forgive me."

When he stepped into the street, he heard that year's first Christmas firework.

⁓

HE THOUGHT IT wouldn't be too hard to get into the school, just a matter of a few minutes and he could run off with his prize. The problem was that he'd always jumped the wall from the inside, never from the outside. The change of direction created several complications, the most important of which was how to keep security guards from seeing him. Fortunately, the two who were on duty that day were on the street, keeping an eye on people's preparations for the Christmas celebration already beginning to take place. The air filled little by little with the explosions of fireworks and the loud music from neighboring houses. The sun had already dipped completely below the horizon, but the warm remains of the day's harsh heat still hung in the air.

Getting over the wall was not as difficult as he imagined. Once inside the schoolyard, he looked at the sky and was struck by the expanse of dark blue, not a single cloud to veil its depths. But he couldn't stop and stare. He knew he was acting like a criminal.

He advanced with his back against the wall and his ear attentive to the movements of the guards. The gloom, which thickened fast, wouldn't let him see whether the shapes that crossed his path were shadows or solid bodies. He rubbed his eyes, trying to force them to get used to the darkness, and continued to head toward the back of the school, to the playground. Soon all that was left was to round the last corner and he would be very close. He looked back and saw the figures of the security guards, leaning over a grill. In the light of the embers, they seemed red devils.

Struck by a sudden blow of terror, he decided to run the last leg. When he slammed against the chain-link fence run right up to the corner, he cursed himself for hurrying and not looking well. Before, the mesh hadn't been flush against the building. This was an unplanned obstacle, but it was already too late. Not only had the fence kept him from continuing on his planned path, but his impact had made a massive ringing noise that had alerted the guards.

Fast as a rat, he slipped into a metal barrel. The bottom was full of dry cement and there were a few rags and newspapers that smelled strongly of chemicals. He curled his small body in the bottom of the cylinder and covered himself as best as he could with the rags and paper. He prayed he could put up as long as necessary with the smell that was burning his nostrils. He shifted a couple of times, looking for the best position in order to stay completely still. When he was about to adjust his arm, which had begun to tingle, he heard the steps of one of the guards approaching.

"What was it?" the other shouted from outside.

"Nothing," replied the one searching in the darkness, waving the beam of his flashlight everywhere, with no rhyme or reason. "Probably just the wind."

He ran his light over the place in the fence where David had hit moments before. Then he briefly illuminated the remains of the construction work that had moved the fence out of place. He breathed in the mountain air and saw his companion still struggling with the coals.

A stream of light licked the edge of the barrel. David squeezed his eyes and body tight, forcing himself once again not to move. The man kicked a random bucket, moved a wheelbarrow, shone his flashlight on the walls, and insisted once again on looking behind the fence, toward the football field.

"Look close!" ordered the one who had stayed outside, after blowing hard into the coals.

"I did," insisted the one with the flashlight. "It had to be the wind."

The guard turned, heading back to the blazing grill.

When he heard those receding steps, David let the air out of his lungs in relief. But when he inhaled again, the chemical-laden air made him cough.

The beam once more played over the top of the barrel, but without stopping to look inside, the guard switched off his flashlight and continued walking away, leaving the body of the boy among the mass of shadows that had taken over.

"Must have been the wind," David heard him mutter as he passed by. "Had to be the wind."

After a while, as stealthy as he could, David uncoiled from the bottom of the barrel. He poked his head up to confirm what he already knew and, once he was sure of being alone, he slowly pulled his numb body free. He gulped anxiously at the clean air, feeling that the chemical smell had permeated his entire body.

To continue, David would have to go back and circle

around the building on the other side. That meant passing just a few yards away from where the guards were stoking the fire for their barbecue. It had been a good try, but he didn't want to be caught. He was afraid of doing something illegal. They could take him to the police, take away his slot at the school for next year, or maybe even take him alone to Social Services. He had to get out of there and far away without anyone noticing. Maybe one of his siblings would have found something to eat.

David had to lean against the wall to keep from falling. He didn't know whether to blame the dizziness on the smell that wouldn't leave his body or the hunger that gnawed at his stomach. He slid down the wall until his butt hit the floor, and he hugged his knees. At least here no one would see him.

The boy closed his eyes and thought that things should be easier. He had misbehaved sometimes, of course, but he had always tried to do everything the right way. He wasn't a bad kid, and when he thought about the unfairness of it all, he wanted to cry. As soon as he felt the tears dripping down his cheeks, however, he thought about how useless and foolish he was being. Not only could he still be discovered, but he had also completely abandoned his mission. He took a breath, remembered the chubby hands of his sister, and stood up, determined to get to the puddle.

Once he was on his way, things were easier than he'd expected. The guards were so caught up in keeping the fire going and drinking their beers, they barely noticed the shadow of his body passing over them. However, after crossing the football field, he realized he had no idea where to start looking. Wanting to slap himself for not thinking it through earlier, he curled up on the ground, growing still and silent so he could hear the frogs croaking.

Whenever he had played in that part of the schoolyard, it had been during the day. Again and again, the ball had wound up in a puddle that never seemed to dry up. Someone told him it was a spring, another boy claimed it was a cursed puddle, and still another laughed at them, saying it must be a broken water pipe.

None of that mattered. Spring or not, if there was water in the puddle, David had to find what he had come looking for. But the night, which blurred all details, complicated things. Determined not to leave without at least trying, the boy crawled a few yards toward the end of the field. He dragged himself through the grass and dirt, imagining how fun it would be to tell Manuela his adventure.

Then his elbow sank into a frigid, wet spot. The puddle! He took the plastic bag from his pocket and dipped it to the bottom of the water. Moving it from side to side, he filled it with liquid and lifted it before his face. Excited, he saw that two large-eyed, long-tailed creatures fluttered in the bag, terrified of their sudden confinement. He took out another bag and carefully transferred the animals to their prison. He repeated the process until, in the dim light of a distant streetlamp, he confirmed the bag was filled with tadpoles.

///////

THE 7:00 P.M. MASS HAD ENDED, and the church was empty. No one but an old woman, who seemed unable to move, remained on the wooden pews. It had been a long time since he'd entered the church. He glanced at the image of Christ and averted his eyes from the expression of intense pain on the figure's face. He remembered that he should feel Him rather than look at Him. He approached the atrium, crossed himself for the second time, kneeling, and closed his eyes with the vague hope of dissolving into the cold, calm air of the church.

The glow of the candles lit to Santa María del Socorro wormed its way through his right eyelid, filling it with red light. He prayed silently, asking for comfort and forgiveness. He explained his reasons, and they seemed even clearer. This was the only escape.

The faces of his brothers and sisters passed before his closed eyes. He explained everything to each of them.

When he finished his prayers, he wanted to remain there in silence for a while, hoping to hear some voice that might give him comfort. But the silence of the church was suddenly filled with the sound of dragging steps: the old woman was leaving. Hector stayed on his knees another moment with his eyes closed until he was filled with the sad certainty that he was alone.

Still, he kept his eyes squeezed tight, and waited a few moments more.

A voice finally spoke.

"We're going to close," it said.

With an unbearable weight in his front pocket, Hector left the church.

Outside, the cold air lit up with the sudden glow of the fireworks.

⁂

HER PINNED-UP HAIR made her seem older. She was holding Manuela's hand, and behind them came Robert, hitting stones with a stick. When they arrived at the store they looked at one another briefly before entering. Maria pursed her lips and paused for a moment, then dragged her two siblings into its illuminated interior.

At the only table a man was sleeping, muttering some incomprehensible song. Doña Carmen lifted her eyes from her sewing when she saw them come in, staring for a moment, then motioned for them to quietly follow her to the back of the house. The three obeyed, trying not to disturb the sleeper. Once they were all in the outdoor washing area, the woman turned on a small light that covered them with a green glow.

"You're so skinny," said Doña Carmen, immediately covering her mouth as if she had said something wrong.

"And our dad?" Robert asked without preamble, and the woman again gestured for him to speak more softly.

"Is our dad coming with presents?" Manuela finished.

Without a word, the woman struggled into a crouch next to the little girl and ran her hand through her hair.

Maria watched her carefully, waiting for her response. Robert instead used his stick to play with the water of the pool. Manuela dodged the woman's attempted caresses.

Doña Carmen opened her mouth, but only a low moan came from her tightened throat. Instead, a slow, dense tear ran down her tanned cheek. In the sky, fireworks exploded, their sparks falling.

With a flash of anger, Maria grabbed her sister and brother and, almost lifting them bodily into the air, rushed out of the store with them, making a great deal of noise.

The drunk, however, didn't even stir.

Doña Carmen looked out the door of her shop, her ample form shuddering as she wiped away the tear that was still running down her neck. She tried to make out the figures of the three children running down the street in the dim light.

All she heard was the din of more fireworks and the loud music thudding from a car going up the street.

She sighed, crossed herself, and went back inside.

〰〰〰

HIS STEPS LED him back to the park. Although he had already made his decision and knew what to do, he wanted to tempt fortune and give rise to one last hope of discarding his plan. He sat waiting for several minutes, who knew how many.

It was fear that made him finally get up and run. A police van stopped in front of the basketball court, and although they were far away, the mere idea that they might stop and frisk him as they usually did made him very nervous. He had to try to avoid getting arrested at all costs.

At first he walked away, pretending to be unconcerned, but as soon as he felt the walls blocking the cops' view, he took off running. His path led him to one of the abandoned lots in the highest part of the neighborhood. Terrified still, he threw himself to the grass, letting the stars get into his head and fill him with little points of light.

Gradually his breathing returned to normal. He brushed his fingers against the weight of the gun pressed against his leg in his pants pocket and decided to change his mind. He convinced himself it was crazy. No one would ever forgive him. Social Services might not be so bad. It would be temporary. Their dad would have to return one day.

Hector got up and walked to one of the trees in the middle of the empty lot. He acted like he was urinating and carefully pulled the gun from his pocket. Once he had it in his hand, he wondered if he should simply drop it or fling it away, then run off as fast as possible.

He stood there for God knows how long, contemplating the decision. The metal grew warm in his hand. His whole body throbbed against it, though he barely registered this. Just when he was thinking of letting the gun pour from his fingers like water onto the ground, not caring anymore about hiding the thing, he was surprised by an arm squeezed around his neck.

"Like pissing on the grass, huh?" snorted the guy, and Hector almost retched at the horrible stench of alcohol. As quick as he could, he slipped the revolver in his pocket.

"Raul?" Hector tried to look back. The hold on his neck loosened, and he turned around.

"Who're you?" the other guy asked, breathing a dozen rancid beers into his face.

"Dude, it's me, Hector. 'Sup?" he said, smiling. "You're so drunk you don't remember."

"Psh, how'm I not gonna remember? I's just screwing with you, bro!" said Raul, smiling. "Whatcha doing here, all by yourself?"

Hector shrugged, wondering whether to tell him, whether to dump on that old drunk friend the whole harrowing story of the last few hours. He looked at Raul, saw the young man squinting through a haze of alcohol, and he knew for certain that he would never tell anyone that he had a gun in his pocket, much less what he planned to do with it.

Unable again to get rid of the thing, Hector's fate was sealed.

"It's Christmas, bro! Let's celebrate!" said Raul. "Nothing bad happens on Christmas!"

Raul put his arm around Hector and pushed him toward the street.

〰〰〰

THE BAG FULL of tadpoles was in the middle of the cooking table. Manuela occasionally pushed her finger against the transparent barrier and felt the weak body of one of the polliwogs bang into it. Maria looked at the bag, tears streaming from her eyes. David had laid his cheek on the surface of the table and was sleepily watching as the movements of the tadpoles got slower and slower.

"What do we do?" asked David, raising his head. His cheek bore the impression of the wood grain.

"We keep waiting?" asked Manuela.

"I . . ." Maria began to say, when the door swung open.

Hector stood in the doorway, a bottle of soda in his hand. He looked at them, smiling.

"Let's celebrate! It's Christmas!" he told his siblings.

"I'm hungry," said David. "Did you bring something to eat?"

"No, but I brought a drink," Hector said, setting the bottle next to the bag of tadpoles. "What's that?"

"Tadpoles. Are they safe to eat?" asked Manuela.

"Are we going to eat tadpoles on Christmas?" Hector laughed.

"They're safe to eat, right?" asked David, looking hopefully at his older brother.

Hector looked at his siblings and suddenly noticed Maria's tears.

"What's wrong with you?" he grunted.

Maria simply lifted the bag in the air.

"Is there nothing else to eat?" she asked.

Hector shook his head and she threw herself on the bed. The table felt very close to his thigh.

"We're going to eat them," announced Hector, pressing his leg against the table so that the metal dug into his flesh. "Better raw than cooked. They'd probably fall apart if we cooked them. Line up!"

The three little ones looked at one another, intrigued, and put Manuela first. Hector opened the bag and emptied the contents into a bowl. Feeling the change in pressure, the tadpoles seemed to revive and waved their tails in a frenzy. With a ladle, Hector served a portion in a cup and offered it to Manuela. She hesitated to take it.

"At least rinse them and change the water," Maria suggested, getting up from the bed, still weeping silently.

Hector nodded, smiling. Once he had them in clear water, the creatures seemed less repulsive. He again served a portion in a cup and, looking into his little sister's eyes, handed it to her. Manuela took it with distrust.

"Can I have soda with it?" she asked.

Hector served her a squirt of soda that mixed with the water and stung the skin of the tadpoles, who squirmed frantically in the new world of bubbles.

"Don't smell it," Robert advised, nudging her from behind. He wanted the ordeal to be over as soon as possible.

Manuela pinched her nose, as if preparing to jump into a pool, then drank the water, swallowing all those slimy creatures. Terrified, she screamed and ran to find her drawer pulled out from under the bed, holding her belly. The others looked at her, smiling.

"Gross?"

"I don't know," said the girl. "I didn't notice. But they keep moving in my belly!"

She curled up in the little drawer. Although her legs no longer fit, she tried to squeeze inside.

"Now you," Hector said to David. Looking at the younger boy's hungry face, he handed him a cup with his portion of tadpoles. David pinched his nostrils and drank the contents without a word. He retched a little, but managed to hold it down as he went to lie down on the bed.

"What do you think?" Hector asked with glee in his eyes. "Any good?"

"I don't know, but I'm not hungry anymore," David confessed.

Robert took his serving and drank it wordlessly too.

"Not so bad," he said, handing the cup back to Hector.

"Now you," the oldest boy told Maria.

"No, I'm not drinking that crap," she declared.

"All of us," Hector growled authoritatively. "Together in everything!"

He handed her a full cup. The girl drank it without looking and, like the others, rushed to the bed.

"Your turn, Hector," Maria said pointedly.

"Yes," said Hector dryly. "I'm the last one. Anybody want soda?"

No one answered.

Hector poured himself a cup of tadpoles with soda and swallowed it, taking care not to chew.

"Ugh, that's disgusting!" he said, and lay down next to Maria, who had her face in her hands.

"What's wrong with you?" he asked again, softly, as soon as he could forget the rotten taste left in his mouth.

Maria lifted her tear-streaked face and looked at her older brother. Motioning him closer with her finger, she whispered something in his ear.

Hector pulled away from his sister. She felt he was seeing her for the first time in her life. It was frightening, the way his eyes widened. A barely constrained groan, almost a whistle, escaped his lips, and without taking his eyes off her, he stood up and backed away toward the door.

Maria sat up in bed, watching the door close. She squeezed her eyes, desperate to stop the flow of tears. She wondered how she could pause whatever mechanism had unleashed them. She wanted to hold them in forever.

Then she heard a noise. At first it seemed the croaking of a small frog, but then it became the repulsive sound of someone retching. She opened her eyes and saw that David wasn't in the room. Looking out the window, Maria saw him running through the courtyard, stooped over. He reached the laundry area and vomited into the drain on the floor. When he had expelled the last tadpole, he rinsed his mouth and went back to bed, trembling.

"Coward!" Robert grunted. He'd followed his older sister to the window and seen. "You made us swallow that shit, and then you go and throw it up."

"I didn't mean it! I wasn't trying to throw up," David groaned, apologetic.

"Yeah, sure. Didn't mean it," Maria said bitterly. "You knew. What you wanted was to kill us all."

David opened his eyes and gasped, horrified at what his sister was saying. Bursting into tears, he scrambled under the bed, squeezing to the very back, behind boxes of clothes, where not even the most persistent sunbeam could reach him, where not even the most cunning lightning could illuminate his face. He curled into a ball in that dark nest, closed his eyes, put a wad of chewed paper in each ear, and made a wish:

Let no one ever see me again.

WHEN HE COULD control the shuddering that had seized his body, Hector could feel the slimy touch of the tadpoles in his mouth again. He checked to make sure the revolver was still in his pocket. As he held it in his hand, he guessed it must be midnight because the fireworks had turned the night sky over Bogotá into a conflagration of explosions.

It was impossible to ignore the holy celebration.

He would go in the same order as the tadpoles. Putting his finger on the trigger, he begged forgiveness once more for what he could no longer stop doing.

Five explosions without a single scream blended softly with the bursts of gunpowder that rained from the sky in a brilliant greeting for the Son of God.

22

IT WAS THE FIRST TIME he'd touched me with any affection. I was petrified. We were sitting by the ditch, wearing T-shirts and shorts. He ran the backs of his fingers along my forearm. I got goose bumps all over. That boy had the power to make my heart gallop a thousand miles an hour. He ran his fingers down my arm again and smiled at me. Although the sun was out and everything glowed, his smile was like a door leading into the light.

I felt the tadpole squirming between my fingers. Its transparent tail sparkled with the sun. The day was hot, and we were together. I had trained and was sure I could swallow that tadpole, if that was what he wanted.

"No," he said and let go of my hand. "If you keep the tadpoles in your belly, you die. It happens to everybody, except me."

I stared at him, waiting for him to tell me more, to relieve the suspense I felt, but more than anything wanting him to brush his fingers against my arm again so I could feel the warmth of his touch.

"They told you I'm immortal, right?"

I nodded. There was no point in lying about something we all knew. Besides, I figured whatever united us at that moment was so strong nothing could undo it.

"It's true. The bullets didn't do anything to me. But all my brothers and sisters died," he said, his voice clenching in his throat. I looked at him carefully.

"I was saved because I threw the tadpoles up," he continued, struggling to say the words, his eyes still locked on mine. "Don't eat tadpoles, Nina, if you don't want to die."

I realized that his brown eyes had turned slightly green. Letting go of the slimy thing squirming in my palm, I smiled at him.

I understood. I was the one who had to touch him. Reaching out, I ran my fingertips down his cheek. A thick tear followed the path of my touch.

"I don't want to be immortal. And I don't wish I would die anymore. I just want to be a normal boy," David said in a sobbing rush. With a quick movement he leaned forward and pulled up the bucket where he kept his tadpoles, pouring them back into the water of the ditch.

The creatures quickly disappeared into the shadows and slimy depths. I touched his cheek again and he took my hand in his.

"We should've planted flowers," he said. "Eating flowers doesn't hurt you."

He stood without letting go of my hand. I followed him almost without noticing my own body. It was like being pulled up by his smile.

We stood there, looking at each other for a second. Silvery gleams danced upon his face. I couldn't tell whether it was sunlight reflecting off the water or the happiness I felt. It didn't matter. There were also gleams on my face, and he stared at them too, but I soon realized they were tears.

I was crying for joy.

He took my hands, his lips parting as if to say something, but he closed his mouth without uttering a word.

Then I understood what he had meant to tell me, and I nodded.

ABOUT THE AUTHOR

Francisco Montaña Ibáñez is an award-winning author for children and a professor at the National University of Colombia (IIE). *The Immortal Boy* is his first book translated into English.

ABOUT THE TRANSLATOR

David Bowles is a Mexican American author and translator from South Texas. Among his multiple award-winning books are *Feathered Serpent, Dark Heart of Sky: Myths of Mexico* and *They Call Me Güero: A Border Kid's Poems*; he is also the translator of *The Sea-Ringed World: Sacred Stories of the Americas*, published by Levine Querido. In 2017, David was inducted into the Texas Institute of Letters.

SOME NOTES ON THIS BOOK'S PRODUCTION

The art for the jacket and case was created digitally by Filip Peraić using Adobe Illustrator. The collage art for the interior was created by Richard Oriolo incorporating ephemera from the past, present, and sleight of hand. The text was set by Oriolo in Walbaum MT Std, a typeface designed by Carl Crossgrove, Charles Nix, and Juan Villanueva for Monotype, restoring the designs of early 19th-century German punchcutter Justus Erich Walbaum into a modern serif meant to combine charm and warmth. The display was set in Wide Latin, first introduced in the late 19th-century by English typefoundry Stephenson Blake. The book was printed on FSC™-certified 98gsm Yunshidai Ivory paper and bound in China.

Production supervised by Leslie Cohen and
  Freesia Blizard
Book jacket and case designed by Filip Peraić
Book interior designed by Richard Oriolo
Edited by Nick Thomas

LQ
LEVINE QUERIDO